THREE WAYS TO S

Graham Joyce is the author of nine novels and has won numerous awards for his writing, including four British Fantasy Awards and the 2003 World Fantasy Award for *The Facts of Life*. He teaches creative writing at Nottingham Trent University and lives in Leicester with his wife and two children. *Three Ways to Snog an Alien* is his third children's novel published by Faber.

Praise for *TWOC*:

'The characters are strong, the delicious prose draws you in and Joyce cunningly keeps back little bits of info so that you just have to keep reading.' *SFX Magazine*

A terrific teen novel, *TWOC* [is] sharply observed.' *TES Scotland*

'I can't think of a bad word to say about it . . . *TWOC* is a grip-ping book . . . The story has action, humour, sorrow and one of the best plot twists I am ever likely to read . . . *TWOC* will appeal to any teenager.' *Leicester Mercury*

Praise for *Do the Creepy Thing*:

A compelling, thought-provoking read, undoubtedly creepy but also ultimately an affirmation of the power of integrity . . . A terrific teen novel.' *Guardian*

'This is a tightly written novel with pace and plenty of action, well structured suspense and a satisfying conclusion that avoids the obvious.' *Carousel*

by the same author
TWOC
DO THE CREEPY THING

Three Ways to Snog an Alien

GRAHAM JOYCE

ff

faber and faber

First published in 2008
by Faber and Faber Limited
3 Queen Square London WC1N 3AU

Typeset by Faber and Faber Limited
Printed in England by CPI Bookmarque, Croydon

A CIP record for this book
is available from the British Library

ISBN 978-0-571-23951-1

2 4 6 8 10 9 7 5 3 1

To Ella

1

· · · · · · · ·

Something not right about the new girl. Not right.

I'm in science class watching her, trying to put my finger on *exactly* what's not right about her when Shelly Hobbs from my experiment group turns into me and I back into the table sending test-tubes and a water-flask flying.

'Doogie, oh Doogie you are so DUMB!'

Shelly Hobbs, she of the loudest mouth in the class. No, forget that. The loudest mouth in the school. My mate Matt says there's something sexy about her. I'm not sure what he means. I mean I know what sexy is. Course I do. Everyone does. But I suppose it's all a matter of personal choice.

She's calling me dumb because I've knocked over the jar of water. Well I probably am dumb if I'm honest. I mean I don't get half of the things we do at school. Like right now. We're doing an experiment to prove something fizzes in water. Duh. Science: what is that all about?

Shelly stands with her hands on her hips, still calling me dumb, and I can't think of a quick reply. Shelly has the biggest bazongas in the class and maybe that's why Matt fancies her. Me, I can't see what the fuss is about. Why are bazongas sexy? Don't get it. Don't get it at all. They're just in the way.

'It was your bazongas,' I hear myself say.

'*Wha-at?*' goes Shelly.

Matt is looking at me with his mouth open.

Well, yes. I can't quite believe that I said it myself. I mean I know I *thought* it. But I didn't mean to actually *say* it. It's like an invisible hand reached into my throat and pulled the words out, and no one is more surprised and red-faced than me. I look round, like someone else in the room might have said it. Like it was all the work of a ventriloquist hiding behind one of the science lab benches.

Shelly can't believe it either. I suppose I'm the last in the class to say something like that. 'Doogie, that's just outrageous!'

Matt sniggers. The fourth person in our experiment group is the new girl. Fresh arrived today. She looks at me and I see a light go on in her eyes. She wants to laugh but she doesn't. Instead she turns away and goes to fetch a roll of paper towels. When she gets back she hands me the paper towels so that I can mop up the mess.

'What's going on in this group?' snorts Pinky Lewis. Pinky is the science teach. Called Pinky cos he's pink. Logical really. He has a neat ginger moustache, ginger eyelashes and balls of ginger hair spilling out of his nostrils, like it's poking out of a rip in a sofa. We could have called him Ginger. But we don't, we call him Pinky.

'Small accident,' I say, wiping up.

'It's all in hand,' says the new girl, taking the soggy towels from me and dumping them in the metal waste bin. 'No problem.' And she looks at me again, and there's that light flickering. She hasn't said anything, but I know she's perked up because of what I just said. And in a weird sort of way I think that's why I said it. To make her laugh or something.

That is, I wanted to make that light come on in her eye. I think. Hell, I don't know!

Meanwhile Shelly looks like she might be ready to grass me up and tell Pinky what I said to her. She thinks better of it, which is a relief. School has a big downer on anyone saying anything about bazongas, knickers, knobs and all that; which is a bit of a strain since it's pretty much all of us in Year Eleven ever think about. Well, the boys, anyway. Well, not me. Well not *all* of the time anyway. The girls probably just think about eyeshadow and handbags and cuddly toys.

Now take my friends Matt, Wilko and Tonga. They're all souped up about getting a girlfriend. I'm not so sure it's a good idea. Some of them talk an awful lot. Like Shelly Hobbs. She likes to have her own way. So, say you're going to get a burger with Shelly Hobbs. What should take five minutes is now going to take longer because there will be all this chat: shall we have a drink with that; shall we have a quarter-pounder; if we have a large fries we can share it . . . all that. And you can't say: *get your own fries Shelly*, because that's just plain rude, ignorant, and anyway you have to be kind to girls if you're going out with them, and it's pretty annoying having to be kind when someone's all over your fries.

And not only that, you're going to have to think about onions. Why? Because if one of you has onions the other person has to have onions. Why? Because you might end up snogging, and there's nothing worse than snogging someone who has just sucked down an onion ring when you haven't. What's worse, if you like onions you might have skipped the onions for this very reason and then you never get round to snogging at all. Which is a waste, when you could have had onions.

And then there is the question of what to do together. Say you want to go down to watch United on a Saturday and she wants to go to the cinema. There's a Saturday gone. And say you do go to the cinema and you want to watch *Zombie Inferno* and she wants to watch *Romantic Island*. You know who is going to win. And so you end up watching *Romantic Island*, and that's your Saturday for you.

Take Matt for example. He comes over all weird when Shelly's around. Fidgets. Acts daft. Keeps flicking his hair and making remarks which are meant to be funny but which are not. I feel sorry for him. He's in a state really. He's a good friend and I keep trying to think of ways to help him out of his misery. I think you should do your best by a mate. I mean, I admit I'm no expert but I said I'd tell her for him. Set up a date. But he just went mad. I even offered to go on a date with him to keep him company. But he just didn't want any help.

I've snogged a girl. Plenty. Okay, not plenty. One. It's all right but it's not as good as it's made out to be.

I had this girlfriend once. Kind of. It wasn't official. Well, I didn't exactly go making a public announcement about it. You don't take out an ad in the paper. You don't hire a little plane to trail a banner across the sky. Sometimes you don't even know yourself if it's official. I mean when is it official? After you've had a snog?

On holiday once in Skegness, there was this girl by the sea wall. She was just an ordinary girl – pretty, nice hands, fairly good hair, smelled okay – and she came up and told me I was good-looking and started talking about all kinds of things of no interest, like what's your name, where do you come from, what music do you like. She had nice sandy coloured skin – I dunno maybe she was Spanish or part Indian or something – but she had these coloured fabric bangles on her wrists and I thought it looked sort of cool. Thing is I didn't know what to say to her. My mouth kept going dry so I let her do all the talking. She had an iPod playing in her ear even while she was talking to me. My face kept going red every time she made eye contact. I had to look away a few times, like I was watching for a passing ship out at sea.

Then she asked me if I wanted to walk down the pier with her. I thought, why? Then I thought why not, even though I had other important things to do. So we went down to the pier. She didn't stop talking all the way except to hum a tune that was going on in her ear. When we got there we chucked a few stones in the sea. That was about it. Then she asked me if I wanted to meet her later.

When we met up later it was as if she hadn't stopped talking from the moment I left her. I mean I heard her coming from a hundred metres away. Talking to me, maybe, or to herself. This time her hair was wet as if she'd just had a shower. As for me, I prefer to make sure my hair is dry before I go out. It's up to the individual.

After a bit we stood against the sea wall for a while. She kept ripping out her earpiece from her iPod and sticking it in my ear so I could get a load of whatever it was. I liked her touching me but after about the third time of this I had a sore ear. Then she came right up to me and we snogged.

It was all good. Not great, but all right. I think she must have been sucking mints earlier. I tried to put my tongue in her mouth but she wouldn't let me. I only did it because I wanted to look like I knew what I was doing.

• • • •

I reckon that counts as going out. I mean even if you're talked half to death by a girl it still counts as going out. Anyway the next day she went back to Runcorn so I didn't see her again. I did look up the bus timetables but, you know, Runcorn is a pretty long way.

The girl by the sea wall was a type nine, and Angelica Vinterland, the new girl in class, is also a type nine. As everyone knows there are only nine types of female. Body types and all that. (This is scientific – I read it on the Internet.) Shelly is type three: large mouth, big bazongas, fattish legs. Matt goes for type threes. Angelica is type nine: small bazongas, tall and bony, nervy. I prefer type nine. When I do eventually decide to let someone go out with me it will probably be a type nine.

The spillage is mopped up and Pinky drifts off to supervise another group at the back of the classroom. Angelica and Shelly fill up the jar I've knocked over and we start all over again with the experiment to see what fizzes. Duh.

'No worries,' says Angelica now that the experiment is under way again.

'Right,' I say, 'no worries.'

Then my other mate, fatboy Tonga, sneaks up behind me and hisses in my ear. 'You fancy her.'

He's another good mate, is Tonga. But even so I let fly and graze his scalp with my knuckle. It catches him a light burn. I know this because it takes the skin off my knuckles.

'Hoi!' Pinky shouts from across the class. 'I saw that!'

Tonga rubs the side of his head and gives me an evil grin. 'You do,' he says. 'You're, like, smitten.'

2

• • • • • • • •

Well, I can't concentrate on school and it's not my fault. Every time I look up, she's looking at me. Angelica, the new girl. She pretends not to, and that just makes it worse. That's girls for you: if they're looking at you they pretend they're not; and if they're not paying you any attention they make out that they are.

• • • •

I try to avoid looking at her during French. I don't mind French. Well I admit I can't speak a word of it but we've got this pretty assistant from Paris who at least makes a change from looking at our normal French teacher's moustache, and our normal French teacher is a woman. Angelica can speak confident French. Completely fluent. But let me tell you, it's a trick! She hasn't really learned it at all!

The trick is that her family lived in France for seven years. How can that be fair? Why should she be allowed to be in our French group when she can speak the lingo and all we can do is go *Bonjour Bonjour*? Why should she get her work marked the same as us when she's obviously going to come top? It's so unfair. She should be made to do Russian, say, instead. Makes the rest of us look thick, which is exactly how I do look when the pretty French assistant asks me something in French and all that happens is that my face goes red.

And when I glance round, there she is, Angelica, sucking the end of her pencil and looking at me. She blinks slowly and this time doesn't even try to look away. No embarrassment at all! No, she just blinks at me.

And then, if that's not enough, at the end of the school day, just when all I want is to jump on the school bus and forget all about the jail-sentence of school, when my time is my own, when I can get on my PlayStation or have my tea, she stops me at the school gates.

I mean I can tell she's going to speak to me. I just know it. She's standing leaning against the wall with her legs crossed at her ankles, school bag slung over her shoulder, and even though there's about a hundred thousand kids squeezing through the school gates at the same time I just know she's going to say something.

How do I know? Because of the way she's looking at me. There's a tiny smile on her lips. Well, like the corner of her lips is twisted in half a smile.

She just swings alongside me. I don't say anything and I don't even look at her, but she's walking by my side. I ice up. I can't stop it but my fingers splay out and my arms are like planks of wood at the sides of my body. I don't like it. I don't like that she can have this effect on me. I can feel big knots in my neck muscles caused by keeping my gaze dead ahead. What's more I can see Matt and Tonga further ahead and any minute they're going to turn around and look back and see her walking with me and it's going to be . . . well, you know exactly what it's going to be.

'I can help you with your French,' she says.

'Eh?'

'I said I can help you with your French.'

'What?'

'I said I can help you get better at French. It's not difficult when you get going.'

'What?'

'I am speaking English right now, aren't I? What I mean is it's amazing how with just a tiny bit of practice you can get good at it.'

I stop dead and she stops dead too. The crowd of kids flow round us like water round a rock. I feel my face screw up. 'You what?'

'My God, I give up!'

'No,' I tell her, 'I know what you're saying. But what are you talking about?'

'I'm talking about extra French. So you can get better. It's easy.'

'Yeh, yeh, yeh, I know what you're saying. But what *I'm saying* about what you're saying is why would anyone want to do any more than we have to?'

'Duh! To get better at it?'

'Look, let's get this straight: school to me is like the prison of Alcatraz. I spend all my time dreaming about the bell at the end of the day. I don't think about anything else.'

I turn away and walk faster towards the bus. She walks alongside me. She has to skip every third step to keep up.

'You're funny! You are! But that attitude is why you're bottom of the class at everything!'

'Like I care!'

'Whoa!' she goes, as if I'm a horse. 'Whoa! You mean you don't mind that everyone thinks you're thick?'

'Hey, I'm not thick.'

'I know that. I've seen it. But all the teachers think you are cos you don't try. And all your classmates think you are too. They're laughing at you.'

'Sod off!'

'It's true. And you know it!'

We arrive at the bus stop. The bus is already there, engine ticking over, kids scrambling on like the school building behind them is a sinking ship and the bus is a life raft. 'What's it to you, anyway?'

And she just blinks at me. Slowly. One single blink. Then she hitches her school bag on her shoulder and walks away.

I get on the bus, shaking my head. There's a seat free in front of Matt and Tonga. 'Need sugar,' says Tonga.

I have a Mars Bar in my pocket that I was saving for the journey home, but I give it to Tonga cos he's always hungry. I suppose he's got a lot of fat to support. He unwraps it and sucks it down in one.

'Hey-up,' says Matt. 'Doogie has got himself a girlfriend.'

Well. I give him the knuckle for that.

● ● ● ●

Gets to me though, that jibe about being bottom of the class. It doesn't matter how badly I do at school, or what the teachers think, I'm not thick. I'm just . . . I've got other stuff to think about. More important stuff. But what did get to me was when she said that the others were laughing at me. My classmates.

The thing is sometimes I pretend to be thick. To get a laugh. It usually works. You can make out you're a bit of a dong, and I like making people laugh. But they are supposed to know. I mean if you're a clown in a circus everyone is supposed to know – aren't they? – that the clown takes off his make-up and his funny hat and goes home; and when he gets home he just wants to have his tea and read the paper. He doesn't shovel his dinner down his trousers, or fall over backwards reading the paper, does he? My dad said that it takes the cleverest guy to be the circus clown. But does the audience know that?

But if I say to Matt or Tonga, 'Hey, am I thick?' they will say, 'Course you are, that's why you're our mate.' And we'll have a laugh at that.

But now she's got me worried. Maybe I've spent so much time pretending to be thick that everyone thinks I really am thick. Or maybe even I've made myself thick. That's another thing that my mum used to say when I was a kid: if you keep on pulling that face the wind will change and your face will stick like that. Maybe that's what happened. Maybe the wind changed and I didn't notice.

I dunno. Something's wrong.

I know this: my school grades are all crap.

'Where're you going in such a hurry?' Mum says when I get in from school. 'Your tea is almost ready.'

'Back in a min, Mum.'

I nip upstairs to my bedroom, where I log on to the Internet. It's easy to find a couple of sites where I can do a quick bit of French. I know it's not really me but I have a point to prove. To myself.

I get past the introductions and then they start on directions. How to get to the baker's, that sort of thing. Anyway I give it a go. 'Est-qu'il y a une boulangerie près d'ici?' No no no. And *non* if you like. CBA: can't be arsed. Who needs to ask to go to the baker's? You just go in a supermarket and there's the bread, piping hot from the oven. Why bother asking? You can see a supermarket from several miles away. It's like standing at the foot of a mountain and going, 'Où est la montagne?'

Forget it. Instead of doing French I have a great idea. I'd like to help Matt out of his misery about Shelly Hobbs so I google *How to pull a babe*. You can find out about most things on the Internet and I wonder if anyone who has been through all this before has any advice to offer. Well, loads of interesting stuff comes up. There's one website called DatingTips.com and I give it a pretty good read.

It's terrific! It's written by some older guy who obviously has had one or two girlfriends in his time, and he's just giving away all the secrets of girls! Everything you want to know about the way they think, what they're thinking at any given time, if they're telling the truth . . . it's amazing. He says he *knows the bends in the road*. I think by this he means that he can tell if there's an accident coming round the corner. Anyway he offers all this advice and he's even written a book on the subject which you can buy from him any time if you want to get really good at it. Mainly it's aimed at older guys because it talks about bars and shaving and driving to a date and all that; but I would say the advice is pretty good. I mean, say you're fourteen, it's probably the same advice as if you're twenty-four, isn't it? Maybe it gets different when you're ninety-four, but right now I'd say that it's all useful stuff on there that I can tell Matt.

I log off and go and get my tea. Which, it being a Thursday, is Chinese takeaway.

Dad has finished a job today so he's already home and tucking into his noodles. He's got sawdust in his hair and plaster powder all down his trousers. He's a fishmonger. No, that was just a joke. He's a builder.

'Dad,' I say to him, 'do you think I'm thick?'

'Thick as pig-poo, son, like your old man.'

'Brian,' goes Mum. Like this 'Bryyyyyy-uunnnnn' She sings it. 'That's not very nice, Bryyyyyyy-unnnnn.'

'Well, he did ask me, didn't he?'

'You're not thick, Doogie,' she says. 'You're not thick, you're . . . uncomplicated.'

Dad accidentally snarfs a noodle because it makes him cough. Then he puts down his fork and wags a dusty white finger at me. 'It's your school work, son. If you paid more attention at school you wouldn't be thick. At the rate you're going you'll end up as a bloody builder, like me.'

'I don't see what's wrong with that. Tonga's dad is a university lecturer and you make twice as much money as he does. Wilko's dad writes books for a living and Wilko brings Chippo economy label crisps to school.'

Dad's head swells a bit at this news. He looks at Mum. 'Well, you'll end up like your mum. All beauty and no brains.'

'Bryyyy-unnnnn.'

'Well, it will be no bad thing if you come into the building trade with me. Be a ladder-monkey.'

'Oh Bryyyyy-unnnnn,' Mum says, as if the decision is already made. 'I wanted him to be the first in our family to go to university.'

Dad sucks down a noodle. 'Flying saucers will land on our front lawn before that happens, the way he's going.'

'I don't like this takeaway,' I say.

'Me neither,' says Dad. 'Chuck it away. Let's have some proper junk food.'

3

●●●●●●●

The next day in school, while Smutz the English teacher is banging on about some book we have to read, I have a good hard look at Angelica. While she's not looking at me, I mean. I don't want our eyes to meet. If our eyes do meet, she doesn't look away like any normal person does: she just holds your gaze. It's creepy.

Anyway there is definitely something weird-looking about her. I mean she's pretty enough. She has lovely sandy skin and dark brown eyes but there is something odd about the shape of her face. Her chin is too sharp. And her eyes are almond shaped. I don't mean oriental. What I mean is Angelica's eyes are round at one end and slanted at the other. That's what an almond looks like.

It's like someone made those eyes when they didn't know whether they were making an oriental person or a white person. Anyway it's attractive and off-putting at the same time.

Well, I get caught. Looking at her eyes I mean.

'Why were you looking at me in English?'

You don't expect a girl to come up to a boy while he's in the middle of a football game at break time, just because he's taking his turn between the sticks and go blah blah blah. You don't just go up to a boy when Wilko is about to left-foot the ball over your shoulder. And even if Wilko scuffs his shot and you collect it easily and throw it out to Matt, you don't still keep talking to the boy.

And they say I'm thick!

'You should go over there,' I say, pointing to the bike sheds. 'We're playing football.'

She does as I say. She marches across to the bike sheds and, arms folded, stands there staring at me. What the heck is the matter with her? Hasn't she got any friends? Now it occurs to me that she's waiting for me to finish playing football so that she can talk to me. Well I'm not. I wasn't telling her to wait for me! Now I feel bad that she thinks I'm going to go over and talk to her. Well I'm not because that will just give Matt and Tonga a great time, won't it?

The bell goes to signal the end of break and I troop off with the others, hungry for more education. Mmmmmm. Can't get enough of it. But I can't help glancing back at her and I see her jaw drop open.

She hurries to my side as we go indoors. 'Why the heck was I waiting over there for you? Now we don't have any time to talk.'

'Talk?'

'Yes, talk. We were going to talk about why you were staring at me in English.'

'Staring at you?'

'Yes, staring.'

'Sorry, you're, like, deluded.'

'No I'm not.'

'Yes you are.'

'No I'm not.'

'Yes you are. I wasn't staring at you. I was looking at your eyes.'

And she blushes. Her hackles go down. Her eyelashes quiver, and I think oh God, she's taken that the wrong way. Completely the wrong way. Completely.

'They're sort of weird.' I say, to fix up the point.

'What?'

'Yeh. Neither one thing nor the other. Creepy.' Now the blush on her cheeks fades to be replaced by a plum-coloured bruise. She looks angry. She's only gone and taken that the wrong way too! 'Hang on!' I try. 'What I meant was, I wasn't looking into your eyes. I was looking *at* your eyes. Because they are unusual. And not because they are interesting. Which they are not.'

'Doogie, have you ever heard the phrase: *when you hit the bottom stop digging*?'

Hell, is she looking annoyed with me! So to smooth it over I say, 'What I mean is: are you half oriental. Or something?'

'What if I am? Is that meant to be a racial dig?'

I hold up my hands. 'Calm down! That's not what I meant. I mean it makes you look . . . sort of . . . exotic.' Exotic. I can't believe I've said that. When that word comes out it's no less surprising than as if a silver wriggling fish has popped out of my mouth.

Anyway it seems to have done the trick in calming her down. Phew.

'Do you think so?'

'Oh yes,' I say. 'Exotic, glamorous and mysterious.'

'All right,' she says sharply, 'don't try to be funny.'

'No I meant it!' I say. I think I did. A bit. 'Are your parents foreign?'

Her eyebrows knit. She looks confused for a moment. 'Yes. Well, one is.'

'Where are they from?'

This is a perfectly natural question. If someone is from another country it's polite – though boring – to ask which country they come from. It's only natural. But then something happens. Angelica comes over all weird.

First her eyelids start fluttering again, but really fast. Then she looks away from me, through the window and up at the sky, looking from the corner of those strange almond-but-not-oriental eyes of hers. 'Latria,' she goes. 'My mum is half Latrian.' Or at least that's what I think she says. I don't get time to ask any more because she says, 'Do you want to go out?'

'Huh?'

'It's a simple question.'

Simple question! Like what is simple about that? Firstly I would think that – in this age of feminissity and all that – that girls would have figured out that although they may very well have the right to ask a boy out that you don't actually go ahead and do it. I mean I have the right to walk backwards to school every morning if I want to, but I don't go ahead and do it. Secondly, you don't take a bloke by surprise when he's being polite and asking about whatever country your parents happen to come from. That is just not on. Thirdly, you don't stand there expecting an instant answer to such things. If you are going to be mad enough to ask up front like that, while all his mates are looking back at you and nudging each other, you at least give him a few months to think about his answer.

I feel my face going red. Flaming up. ''Kay.'

Oh no, how did that happen? I meant to say no! I meant to say I can't. And my lips got all twisted and mashed and it came out like I was saying yes! This is a nightmare!

'You know Café Vienna on Echo Lane? See you there at 6.30 tonight?'

She hitches her bag on her shoulder and she's gone. I don't even know how she's talked me into it. I don't even fancy her. Well, not much. I mean she's not exactly my type. I've no idea what's happening or why I've said yes. It's like someone put something in my brain to make me do things I don't want to do.

Somehow I'm going out with the new girl in class.

4

· · · · · · · ·

'They're running an extra French class at school,' I tell Mum by way of explanation.

She nearly drops the Hoover in surprise. Then she does that soppy thing. 'Awwww, Doogie. That's lovely, our Doogie. And just think: it'll come in handy if you ever need to speak French, won't it?'

The best way to deal with my mum is just to blink and say nothing. I'd die for her and I love her to bits but she's a drip. Anyway I certainly wasn't going to tell her that I was on my way to meet a girl. *Awww, our Doogie, with a girl, that's lovely. She'll come in handy to go to the pictures with, won't she?*

Another way to stop her asking too many questions is to ask her for money. 'Can you lend me a few squid, Mum?'

'Again? Our Doogie! I don't know what you do with it.' But she finds her purse and gives me a fiver. 'Make that last you the week.'

I kiss her. Mums are easy.

Before leaving I've got time to go into the bathroom, lock the door and splash a bit of my dad's aftershave lotion on my cheeks. Not that I shave. I chuck a bit in my armpits too, in case my deodorant isn't strong enough. A mistake, cos it makes my armpits itch, but it's done.

Quick mirror scan. Zit check – clear. Bogie check – don't wanna get caught with one of them chaps clinging to the nostril – clear. Bits of cress stuck in the teeth – clear. I've been getting a build-up of ear wax lately but it looks okay. Not that she's going to look in my ears but you don't want it to seem like you've got last year's Christmas cake in your sound vents. I comb my hair backwards but it makes me look like a TWAT! I say that in the mirror: YOU TWAT, DOOGIE! So I comb it forward. It's not much better, still TWATTY, but it's going to have to do.

Bus to Café Vienna. It's only a few stops and when I get there she's waiting outside. This is a nuisance. I was hoping to get there first so I could, you know, arrange myself. I mean pick a decent table. Now we'll have to go in and sit down in a rush.

'Hi,' I say. She looks a bit weird cos I've never seen her without her school uniform on. She's wearing jeans with a huge belt and buckle and showing her midriff. She's looking at me strangely. Almond yes, yeh yeh, we've been through that. But there's something not right about those eyes.

'Hi.'

I stop there. The back of my neck is itching, so I scratch it. I'm not sure what to do really. Do we shake hands? Nah. Peck on the cheek? Nah. Jokingly grab bum? Nah. Oh my God. 'Hi,' I say again.

'Hi.'

Then it's like this force is tempting me to say Hi a third time. I have to fight it back. It's like some creature inside me is trying to get me to say Hi just to make me look a twat.

She points a pinky at the door. 'Are we going in?'

I nod. She walks in front of me.

'Let's sit at the back,' she says.

At the back of the café there are these cool booths with western-style doors, so you can be semi-private. But it's all a bit obvious if you ask me. You might as well wear a badge saying: we're going to try for a snog! So I say, 'No, let's sit in the window.'

She shrugs. 'Okay.'

There's another reason why I don't want to follow her suggestion and sit in the booths at the back. I've read all about this on that site DatingTips.com that I was looking at for Matt. Here's what it said:

Girls prefer a guy to be confident and decisive. So don't wring your hands asking her where she wants to sit. Even if she suggests a particular table, she's probably testing to see if you can really call the shots. So choose a table and lead her there. Be clear about who is in charge and you'll save yourself a lot of hassle later on. She'll appreciate that.

So basically when the girl suggests something, like let's sit at the back, you have to say no, let's sit at the front, so that she can admire how confident you are.

The waitress comes up. Not a word, just holds her pencil over her pad. 'I'll have a cappuccino,' Angelica says.

'No,' I say, 'we're both having ice-cream.'

'Huh?' says Angelica. 'I'd rather have a coffee.'

I look at the waitress. Her nostrils twitch. Otherwise no movement. 'Look, I'm paying. It's my treat, so I say what you have.'

The waitress turns her head a fraction to face Angelica, and I see her eyebrow go up slightly. Angelica looks at the waitress, then looks back at me, and *her* eyebrow goes up fractionally, too.

'All right,' I say, 'you can choose any kind of ice-cream you want. Me, I'm having a Mint Chocolate Chip.'

Angelica shakes her head a little, then lets a jet of air pass between her teeth. 'Okay, I'll have a Neapolitan.'

'That okay with you,' says the waitress, 'if she has a Neapolitan?'

'Yeh, it's fine,' I say.

'It comes with a spoon and a wafer. Is that okay for her, too?'

'Yep. That's okay.'

The waitress goes off with our order.

Another thing it said on DatingTips.com was this:

Don't flirt with the waitress, and when ordering, be decisive. Let the waitress know you're the kind of guy who knows what he wants and who won't settle for less. Being firm with the waitress in this way will have the effect of impressing your date. She'll see how confident you are in dealing with females in general.

It's full of good stuff like that, which you wouldn't have thought of yourself. I'm not doing this DatingTips.com thing for myself. I'm just researching it all and testing it out so I can help Matt. I'm planning to report it all back to him.

'You okay?' says Angelica.

'Yeh. Are you?'

She nods. 'Ça va bien.'

'Eh?'

'We're going to do French, aren't we?'

'What?'

'Isn't that why we're here? To speak French? To improve your French?'

Can you believe it? This is why girls drive you mad. She

can't be in any doubt this is a date. You know, a boy-girl thing. But she has to pretend it isn't. And I have to pretend I don't know she's pretending; and we both have to make out like this is all about me getting better at French. In fact I knew this already, because it did say more about it on DatingTips.com.

> Remember this: girls are just as crazy for guys as we are for them, but they hate to admit it. In fact they will go to staggering lengths to avoid revealing that they have the hots for you. But trust me: if you've got her as far as a restaurant date, then you're already three-quarters to where you want to be. She's hot to trot, but you're going to have to play it as if you're both just there for a pleasant round of conversation. That's the deal.

So it's saying that girls often want to get into your pants but they don't want you to know, so they put up this big smoke-screen. So that's why we all end up speaking French when we don't want to.

I'm just staring at Angelica because I don't know what to say in any language: English, French or Congolese.

She looks at me hard, pretending to be puzzled. 'So why did you think we were here?'

All right. All right. Trick question. And I'm not falling for it. This is so I can be the one to admit that we're on a date. Then she can roll her eyes and go: *date? date? what date?* Then I'm the one who looks like a complete tosser! So I'm supposed instead of that to say, yes I'm here for the French. And that way she's got me into her system of stringing this all out pretending that she doesn't fancy me at all.

Out of the corner of my eye I see the waitress coming with our ice-creams. Just before she arrives I say, 'Well, I'm just here for an ice-cream.'

Angelica bites her thumb and searches me with those mysterious deep brown eyes of hers. She's got half a smile on her face. 'Good answer,' she says.

'Is it okay if she has this ice-cream now?' says the waitress.

'Yes,' I tell her. 'That will be fine.'

• • • •

Things go well enough. I mean there are none of those silent moments when no one can think of anything to say. She's a fast talker and I can always make people laugh so we don't get any time to think: is this date going well? If you think: is this date going well, then it isn't going well, is it? Though every now and then she does go back to this French thing and tosses in a few words. Which is annoying. Not really annoying. I don't get furious about it or anything like that. Just mildly annoying.

I answer her in a made-up language. I say things like: *jolly ma banjo, et tu?* But it doesn't throw her. Turns out she can speak fluent German AND Japanese, too. Her dad has moved all round the world with his job. Something high-powered to do with Information Technology. He's a computer software wizard, and everywhere he's worked, Angelica has gone with him, acquiring all these languages as easy as getting a stamp in your passport.

I think I would like to kiss Angelica. She's strange-looking but pretty. When we go our separate ways I'm going to wipe my lips and go full on for a tonguey. It's the only way to clear up whether this is or isn't a date. On second thoughts I might not go for the full tongue. Maybe just pop in the tip. I haven't decided yet.

After about half an hour or so she suddenly says she's got to go. It takes me by surprise. I thought dates were longer than half an hour. Say about ninety minutes minimum. Anyway she says she's got to get back.

'You haven't finished your ice-cream,' I say. I don't mind, but I am the one paying, after all, and there's still a bit of melted Neapolitan in the bottom of the fancy glass it came in.

'I have to go. My folks don't like me staying out.' Her pullover is draped across the back of the chair. She picks it up and pulls it over her head. 'Walk me to the bus stop?'

'Okay.' I stand up and go over to the till and pay the waitress. The ice-creams come to three-twenty and when I offer the fiver the waitress tells me she's short of change and asks if I have the twenty.

I haven't, so I turn to ask Angelica to see if she has it, and that's when I see it, in clear view.

She's finishing off her ice-cream, but she doesn't see me looking. Her hair is falling over her face but I can see her licking the bottom of the ice-cream glass, with her tongue.

And her tongue is at least a foot long. Longer.

It's like a long, thin, red lizard's tongue. It's forked at the end and it laps at the melted ice-cream. Then this long, long tongue rolls back in a coil into her mouth.

'Well?' says the waitress.

I look back at her. I'm lost for words. I shake my head and look back at Angelica.

But now she's replaced the empty ice-cream glass on the table and is smiling back at me, waiting for me to finish the transaction with the waitress so we can go. But I can't move. The muscles in my legs have turned to slush. The room spins.

'I'll let you off the twenty pence,' says the waitress, 'if you promise to go easy on your girlfriend.'

'Eh?'

'Nothing.' She gives me two quid change.

'Hurry up!' says Angelica. 'I'll miss my bus.'

We hurry to the bus stop without a word, though Angelica occasionally flashes me a smile over her shoulder as we step out the couple of hundred metres. When she does this I can't help staring in the vicinity of her mouth, searching for signs of that long lizard tongue.

When we get to the bus stop she says, 'What's wrong?'

'Nothing.' It comes out too fast. 'Nothing.' But now I can't help staring at her mouth when she opens it to speak.

Her lips look perfectly normal; her lower lip plump and glossy and her upper lip a little thin. Nothing unusual there. She smiles at me again. She has a nice white set of teeth, but no hint of the coiled horror that lives in her mouth. I look closely at her skin, to see if there are any scales, anything reptilian, but there's nothing.

'You sure you're okay?'

'Yeh.'

She takes a step closer. I know she thinks I'm going to make the move to kiss her.

'No frigging way!' I yell.

She laughs. Then knits her eyebrows? 'What?'

I try to laugh it off. 'Nothin'. Jus' kidding.'

'But what did you say?'

To my relief the bus comes hurtling round the street corner. It draws alongside us and the doors wheeze open. Luckily for me I'm going the other way. She gets on. She shakes her head at me, bewildered. 'See you tomorrow then?'

'Yeh,' I say, and I turn, stalking rapidly away from the bus stop. I can tell she's watching me. Even as I hear the bus pull away behind me I can tell she is observing me, scanning me, measuring me up.

5

●●●●●●●

'Go on then, our Doogie!'

It's Mum, when I get back. She's standing in the kitchen, blocking my path. She has her hands on her hips and she has this big sloppy smile painted on her face.

'What?'

'Go on then, our Doogie! Speak it! Speak French!'

I colour up. 'Bonsoir, Maman. Comment allez-vous?' It's all I've got. All I can remember.

'Awwwwwwww! Our Doogie! Speaking French! Awwwwwww! Say it again.'

I repeat the words over for her.

'What's it mean?'

I tell her. She tries to move her lips along with me when I'm saying the words. Luckily I know that she won't ask me to say any more than that. To be honest it would be too much for her to think about at one time. It's sad really. I love her but like I told you, the truth is my mum is thick. I never know whether to kiss her or have her put in a home.

'Awwww. Moman? Is that me?'

'No, you're Maman, not Moman.'

'Awwww, lovely.' Then she pinches my cheek between her thumb and forefinger, something she's been doing since

I was three years old.

'Mum! Gerroff!!!'

'Ha! You dint say that in French, did ya? Eh, our Doogie? Did ya?'

I shake my head and trudge up the stairs to my bedroom.

Right, the first thing that any normal person would do on seeing someone flick a lizard tongue at an ice-cream bowl would be to tell someone else. But who am I going to tell?

I can't tell my mother on account that 1) I've lied to her about going to French classes, not to mention fleeced her for a fiver to buy ice-creams, and 2) I'd have to explain that I've been on a date and I'd never hear the end of it and Angelica would be invited round for the jam sponge and cup of tea, and 3) you've seen how thick she is, so the information that I've been on a date with a girl with a lizard's tongue would overload her brain and she'd drop dead from vibration.

I can't tell my dad either for reasons 1 and 2, and because, 3) I'd have to endure days and days and days of 'Here comes Romeo' and 'Look out, it's Coventry's answer to Casanova!' type remarks. A pain after the first three thousand times of hearing them. Not to mention the lizard's tongue would only have him saying, 'Have you been at the whisky cabinet?' or worse he'd say, 'Geercha!' and cuff my ear for taking the mickey.

I can't text my mates Matt, Wilko or Tonga because if I did I'd also have to reveal that I've been on a date with . . . the *thing* . . . and this time much mickey would be taken in the other direction.

I go upstairs to my room, log on to an Internet search engine and type in the words *lizard tongue*. Holy Moses! The first thing that comes up is a site where you can have your tongue split by surgery! Yeh! *Yeh!* How messed up is that? Now maybe that's an explanation, but I don't think so. I can't imagine a fifteen-year-old girl going in for that tongue-slitting surgery. I don't even want to think about it. And anyway it wouldn't account for the coiled rope of tongue that went back into her mouth after she'd polished off her Neapolitan, would it?

Then there are tons of sites about lizards. Which is what you'd expect. I mean real lizards, desert lizards, jungle lizards, Australian blue-tongued lizards . . . but nothing that talks about people with lizard tongues, so I give up the search.

But in bed I can't stop thinking about it. In fact I wake up in the middle of the night thinking about it. I don't much like the way that Angelica, with her lizard tongue, can come into my dreams.

I don't like it at all.

• • • •

Next day at school I decide to play it normal. And cool. I avoid eye contact with Angelica during lessons. I choose to sit well away from her, too, but in a position where I can watch.

There's no sign of the tongue. When she's writing, she compresses her lips together. Same as when she's listening to the teacher at the front of the class. Now if that were Tonga it would be different. Tonga just can't seem to keep his tongue in his mouth.

When he's writing, Tonga has his head on one side and his tongue drools out like a bloated and blubbery red maggot.

But I'll say this for my mate Tonga's tongue: it's not

forked, and it's not coiled and it's not a foot long. Not like someone's I could mention.

She comes up to me in the school yard. I'm trying to play footie again.

'Are you ignoring me?'

'Ignoring you? Why would I ignore you?'

'I don't know,' she says hooking a dark curl with a pinky and parking her hair behind her ear. 'You just seem a bit off.'

'A bit off?'

'Yeh. I dunno.'

'No, I'm not off. I'm on.'

'Come over here a minute then.'

I walk away from the game. Matt and Tonga are hooting behind me, where you going with her and all that crap. We head towards the bike sheds. I lean my back against the brick wall. She stands facing me with her arms folded.

'That's okay then,' she says. 'It's probably just me. I just had a hunch you were cross with me or something.'

'As a matter of fact,' I say, 'I want your help. I'm doing what you said: trying harder at school. I'm conducting a scientific experiment. For science class.'

She wrinkles her nose. This might be true, because we've all been asked to come up with a study area that we have to research. 'So what is it?'

'Right. One in four people can't roll their tongue. Like this.' And I stick out my tongue, but rolled, exactly the way one in four people can't do. I'm one of the three in four people who can. Obviously, or I wouldn't try this. 'And I'm going to make a study of it.'

She looks suspicious. Her dark eyebrows knit hard. 'What's the point of that?'

'Science, isn't it? Can you do it?'

'I mean if you've already found out that one in four people can't do it, then it must have been researched already. So what's the point of doing what's already been proved?'

'Never mind that. Can you do it?'

'But my point is why not do something that hasn't already been tested or proved? That's much more scientific than just copying someone else's study.'

'Look, can you roll your tongue or can't you?'

'You're not listening to what I'm saying!'

'Show me.'

'Listen! I'm saying you can come up with something much better than that. Something that will impress the teacher.'

'Just show me your tongue.'

'What about the point I'm making?'

'Go on.'

'What?'

'Show me. Go on. Show me.'

'No!'

'You don't want to, do you?'

'Not now I don't, no.'

'Just bloody well show me your tongue! You don't have to roll it! Just show me your tongue!' I was shouting by now: I admit it.

'No, I bloody well won't.'

'There you are then!'

'There you are what?'

'That's got you!' I said. 'Hasn't it!'

'You're mad! Completely mad!'

'Point proved,' I say smugly, nodding at her. 'Point well proved.'

Angelica shakes her head and storms away.

I see very little of her for the rest of the day. She keeps her distance and I don't see her at home time either. I guess that's it. We aren't going out together any more. We're probably the first couple to split up because a girl won't show a boy her tongue.

I've managed to end our relationship, but I haven't solved the mystery.

6

· · · · · · ·

We don't actually speak to each other for the next two days. It's quite easy to keep out of each other's way if you want to. And that would have been that if Matt hadn't stuck his beak in.

One or two members of the class are maybe getting a bit frustrated by the lavish praise Angelica is earning from every single teacher. It isn't that she's a swotty type – she doesn't parade her superiority in every subject, she isn't a mite too quick to answer questions in class like some people I could mention. She keeps her head down. It's just that you get a bit tired of hearing it.

'Angelica, you're way ahead of this stuff,' says Rhino Robertson, the huge bald sweating bulk whose job it is to teach maths. It seems like the overhead lights make his bald head sweat and shine at the same time. The stuff just pours off him. 'We might have to think about moving you up into the sixth form. This stuff isn't even challenging you.'

This stuff isn't even *challenging*? Right. This stuff as he calls it is the black arts. Tangents and sines and cosines. Another foreign language. I showed it my dad, who went, 'Bloody Nora!' This is what we have to put up with these days. Older people, like my dad, all they had to do was divide twenty-four apples between six people, stuff like that. I don't think it's fair.

Anyway, apart from speaking French and Japanese and being a whiz at IT and brilliant in English and talented at Art and Design, she goes at this Maths stuff like a Rottweiler chewing a baby's arm.

Anyway Matt gets all mouthy. 'How come,' he says to her loud enough for everyone in class to hear 'if you're so bright you're going out with my mate Doogie?'

This gets a few laughs. Normally I'd just laugh along with it, but I'm beginning to change my way of thinking about that. I look at Angelica to see what she has to say to him in return. But she doesn't say anything. She just does what any five-year-old kid would do: she sticks her tongue out at him, and then gets on with her work.

A perfectly ordinary, quite pretty, silky little pink tongue. No fork. No coil. Normal.

Right. Right. Okay, so either I've made a prize dick of myself; or something else is going on. You see there was something in the way she looked at me just after she stuck her tongue out. As if she was saying, see, it's normal.

But why would you do that? I mean if it were normal you wouldn't expect anyone to think it other than normal, would you?

Okay, maybe I'm completely wrong. Maybe I have made a fool of myself. Maybe I owe her some sort of an apology.

● ● ● ●

At the end of the school day I wait for her as she comes out of class. 'Hey!' I say.

She ignores me. Hitches her bag on her shoulder and quickens her pace. I think that's a bit rough. When a bloke goes hey and you don't even say hey what. *Hey you, hey who, yeh you, who me, yeh you, yeh what.* None of that. Just carries on like she hasn't heard me.

I catch up with her. 'What's the big hurry?'

She stops dead in her tracks, turns and fixes me with big brown angry eyes. And says nothing. Not a word.

What's a bloke supposed to do about that? Her eyes are, like, boiling. Big bubbling witches' cauldrons of black tar. She glares at me and I feel my cheeks on fire. I want to laugh. 'What?' I say.

'What do you mean, what?'

'I mean what.'

No answer again. Just glares at me with those hot, moist eyes, compressing her lips at the same time. Other kids are filing past us, getting an eyeful of this nothing happening between me and Angelica.

'I just thought I'd . . .' I let my words tail off. Partly because I feel idiotic, partly because I haven't actually got anything to say.

She folds her arms and crosses her legs at the ankles. Her eyes still burn into me. This is what I mean about girlfriends. I'm not even going out with her and it's like having your arms tied behind your back and having your head pushed into a huge tub of marmalade.

'Do you want to meet again?' I hear myself saying.

A little twitch of the head but no answer. No answer! Eyes still boiling in her head.

I try again. 'Café Vienna.' I don't know why I'm even trying. She's still furious with me. It's not like she's going to say yes, is it?

'What time?'

'Eh?'

No answer. Arms folded even tighter.

'Seven,' I say.

'And if I want a coffee this time?'

I hold my arms wide and shake my head slowly. 'I've got nothing against you having a coffee. Nothing at all. Nothing in this world would give me more pleasure than if you were to have a coffee. There's no reason –'

'Oh shut up. See you at seven.'

And she's gone.

Well, what are you supposed to make of that? In DatingTips.com it tells you how to read a person's body language, which is a cool way of knowing what girls are really thinking. For example if a girl touches her ear lobe while she's talking to you, she really wants to play with your willy, that sort of thing.

> Body language is a sure-fire way of tuning into a girl's innermost thoughts. Are her arms folded? She's feeling defensive towards you. Back off! Are her feet pointing away from you? You've lost her attention! But if she's making eye contact with you and flicking back her hair, you're on to a winner!

Well that can't be right. Because there was Angelica with her arms folded and looking at me like I was a dog turd and then she goes and says yes she will see me later. Explain that one for me if you can

Whatever, it looks like we're going out again.

● ● ● ●

When I get to the Café Vienna she's not there, even though I'm bang on time. The place is a bit busier tonight but the seat by the window where we were last time is free, so I slide in there.

Note how I avoid the booths at the back again.

The same waitress is working. She's busy taking someone else's order. Tonight she's wearing a very short skirt, which is not a good idea because she has these huge thighs. I mean the sort of thighs that could be used to strangle a man, if she were the strangling type.

The waitress comes across to me with a jaunty swing, pencil and pad at the ready. 'Oooh,' she says, 'if it isn't mister masterful. How are we tonight?'

'We're good.' I say. 'I'll just have a coffee. Please.'

'What kind? Espresso? Cappuccino? Latte?' She swings her hips when she says these things. Espresso; swing. Latte; swing. There's a painting on the wall of Vienna by night. I keep my beads fixed on that so that my gaze doesn't accidentally stray to those massive pink thighs.

She puts the menu card flat on the table. With a flamingo-painted fingernail she taps the list of coffees. I'm going to have to look at the list and hope that my eyes don't take in her thighs as my gaze switches from Vienna by night to the menu.

I go to check out the list and then — bugger! — my eyes take in her thighs just for a split second, even though I don't want them to! I knew that would happen. I can see her smirking at me. She flicks back her bleach-blonde hair and says, 'Take all the time you want.'

Then she stands there pulling at her ear lobe with her finger and thumb and I feel a rush of blood to my face. My cheeks are burning like hot embers! My ears are steaming! It's embarrassing to be so embarrassed. And the waitress is leering at me like she's won.

'Just ordinary thighs,' I blurt.

'What?'

'Ordinary coffee. I said just ordinary coffee. Ordinary ordinary ordinary.'

Her eyebrows knit for a moment. Then she shrugs and takes her huge thighs away, thank God. And in the same moment Angelica arrives.

'You okay?' she says, sliding into the seat opposite me. There's something odd about her but I haven't figured out what it is yet. More odd than usual, I mean. An extra layer of oddness.

'Yeh,' I tell her. 'It's that waitress. Thunderthighs. Don't look!'

Too late! Angelica looks across at the waitress. Now the waitress knows I'm talking about her.

'What about her?'

'She's been flirting with me.'

'Really?'

'Yeh. Trying to get me to look at her legs.'

Angelica laughs. 'Are you sure?' There's certainly something different about her tonight. I can't put my finger on it.

'Perfectly sure.'

'How do you know?'

'Body language.'

'Tell me.'

So I start telling Angelica about body language and how you can tell someone's real feelings by looking at their body. I'm just about to mention DatingTips.com and I stop myself, because it's not a good idea to tell her that I've been reading up on what to do on a date, in case she now thinks I've got an unfair advantage. When the truth is I was looking at DatingTips.com for Matt, not for myself.

'Why did you stop?' she says.

'Eh?' I often say *eh?* even when I've heard perfectly well, because it's a useful tricksy way of getting an extra moment or two to think up your answer. 'Eh?'

'You stopped halfway through a sentence. Why was that?'

'No, I didn't.'

'Yes, you did.'

I look at her and I finally see what it is that's so diff. Her face is plastered with make-up. I can't think why I didn't see it before but now it hits me full force. It's like seeing someone with a new haircut. You know there is something about them but you don't know what it is. My dad had a goatee beard for years and when he shaved it off my Gran kept asking him if he'd lost weight, which was ridiculous. How much can a few goatee hairs weigh?

But now I look at Angelica she's got an orange face, blue eyelids and lipstick that makes her mouth look like she's been eating blackberries in September. I'm not keen. What if we want to snog later? Not that I do, but if we go ahead then what am I gonna do with all that stuff coming off on my face? It's going to look like I got pasta sauce all down my shirt.

'What's up?'

'Nothing.'

'You look like you've seen a ghost.'

The waitress, old Thunderthighs, gets me out of this little difficulty by arriving with her pad and pencil. Now it's a struggle between glancing at those terrifying thighs or blinking at Angelica's hideous make-up. I hide from both in my old safe harbour of Vienna by night. 'She'll have a coffee,' I say.

'No, I want an ice-cream,' Angelica says.

'This could be interesting,' says the waitress.

I look at Angelica. When we were at school she told me she definitely wanted a coffee. 'You said you wanted coffee.'

Angelica shakes her head. 'Can change my mind, can't I? I liked that ice-cream I had the other night. I want it again.'

'I wouldn't let her get away with that,' says the waitress. She's got a straight face but I've got a sneaking feeling she's taking the mickey out of me. The thing is this: I've only got exactly the right money for us to have a coffee each. If Angelica has an ice-cream I'm sunk. I won't be able to pay the bill.

'Mint chip,' says Angelica.

The waitress writes that down, but spends a long time doing it, pronouncing the words loudly and in a thick voice as if she's five years old. 'Choc. O. Late. Min. T. Chi. P.' Then she looks at me. Will that be all right, sir, if the impudent young lady has her chocolate mint chip?'

'Fine,' I say, but it comes out in a squeaky voice, so I say, 'Yes.' And off she goes.

Now I'm worried about the bill.

Let's be clear about who is paying the bill: you are. No discussion about going dutch or sharing the bill should be tolerated. You are sending out a strong message to say: I can provide for you. I am a man with the wherewithal. I am a man with resources. You should certainly not compromise that message in the early stages of dating.

In fact DatingTips.com recommends you always pay the bill on your first three dates. I don't know why it stops at three. Perhaps it's to trick the girl into thinking that you're not a skinflint or anything like that. Anyway, you're not going to get anywhere, according to DatingTips.com if on the first two meetings you come out looking like you're as tight as a camel's arse in a sandstorm. I don't know if I agree with this, but DatingTips.com seems to think that females can't think of anything but money money money.

> Nice girls are never going to admit this but the fact is that money talks, hardship walks. If you don't flash the cash, they're pretty soon down the road with some butt-ugly guy who owns a Porsche. Get used to it. So even if you don't have it, well make it look like you do. Cash: if you can't shake it, you better fake it.

Which isn't great because now I'm thinking how I'm going to face sarcastic Thunderthighs with not enough to cover the bill.

'Anyway,' Angelica says, 'it's my treat this time.'

'What?'

'It's my turn to pay.'

'Eh?'

'You paid last time. It's my turn tonight.'

'No,' I hear myself saying. 'I can't let you do that.'

'Why not?'

'Because I'm paying.'

'You sure?'

'I'm sure I'm sure.'

She shrugs. 'Okay.'

'That's settled then.'

The ice-cream comes. 'Want another coffee?' the waitress asks me.

I do want another because my first coffee cup is empty. But I haven't the money, so I say, 'No, I never have a second cup.' I don't know why I say that. I don't want anyone to guess that I don't have the dough.

Angelica gets stuck into her ice-cream. I try not to look at her mouth as she spoons it in. I mean all that lizard tongue thing is over, pretty much. But you can't help looking. I wouldn't mind if she spilled a bit on her hand and had to lick it, just to put my mind at rest, but she doesn't. Just then I notice that on the menu it says that the price of a coffee includes a refill.

'What you thinking about?' says Angelica.

'I think I will get another coffee after all.'

'Thought you never drank a second cup.'

'Well, the first cup was only really half a cup,' I say, getting out of my chair.

I have to walk all the way to the back of the café. There the waitress is standing just inside the kitchen, joking and laughing with the chef, holding the door ajar. I tap her on the shoulder and she looks round, startled. The chef shuts up too, and stares at me. 'I will have a second cup after all,' I say. 'Coffee.'

She nods. I turn away and make my way back towards my seat. Then I go back to the waitress and say, 'I'm a bit thirsty today.' The chef looks at me, then he looks at the waitress.

I make my way back to Angelica, who is also looking at me a bit oddly. I slide into my seat.

'Ça va?' she says.

'Oh bloody hell, don't start that again!'

'That's why we're here!'

'Don't start that again, either!'

She's just about to reply when a black shape flings itself at the window of the café. Then another black shape.

It's Matt and Tonga. They've pressed themselves up against the window, arms spread wide, their noses squashed against the glass like fat, pink snails. Angelica laughs, like that's funny. My God, that's so old, doing that. It's something you do when you're, like, five, or maybe seven at the most. But she's laughing like it's a fresh new all-round big-time joke.

'How did they know we were here?' I ask.

'I certainly didn't tell them.'

They must have been prowling around since school time because they're still wearing their school blazers. Then I think, oh dammit, they're coming in.

And come in they do. They seem to fill the place. Other folk sipping their coffee and nibbling their cakes and sucking their lettuce look up uncomfortably at these two louts. Matt has a hungry, wild-eyed gleam in his eye and Tonga has his tongue out as usual, and the pair of them look like they might just go round the café licking the crumbs off the tables.

'What's goin' on here then?' says Matt. He slides into the seat next to me. Tonga is too bloody fat to do the same next to Angelica. He just stares at her, licking his lips. That's Tonga.

'What's going on?' I say. 'What do you mean what's going on? We're having a coffee that's what's going on.'

'We're doing extra French,' says Angelica.

Matt has a short, dirty laugh. More like a bark. No, more like a rifle going off but muffled by his mouth. It sounds like this: *brap*! 'Brap! That's a good one! Brap! Hear that, Tonga?'

'French,' says Tonga. 'Très bien.'

'You look very cosy together, if you ask me.'

'Yeh, well, we weren't asking you,' I say.

Tonga has already lost interest. He's eyeing everyone's food again. Then the waitress appears with my second cup of coffee. 'Hello, boys. What are you having?'

'Get us a coffee, Doogie. I'm skint.'

'Me too,' says Tonga. 'Get us a coffee.'

'You treating them, then?' ask the waitress.

Now I'm in a hole. I want Angelica to think I'm generous and I probably would buy them a drink if I had the dosh, but I haven't. 'We're leaving pretty soon,' I say.

'Are we?' says Angelica.

The waitress looks at me and something like sympathy passes across her face. She looks at Matt and Tonga and says, 'Well, boys, that sounded like a no.'

Tonga licks his lips again. And then he looks at the waitress's fat thighs, like FULL ON. Like he might fancy a slice on a sandwich. Jesus. Matt tries to look cool. 'We'll just stay here and keep you company.'

'I don't think so,' says the waitress with a ferocious smile. 'No pay no stay.' And she jerks her thumb at the door. Matt and Tong, meek little kittens, sigh and get up to leave. Though Tonga lets out this prize loud burp on his way out.

'See you love-birds in class,' Matt shouts on his way through the door.

But at least they're gone.

'That's one you owe me,' says the waitress with a wink.

I feel a bit embarrassed. But I look at Angelica, and I wonder if her and the waitress are in this together, somehow. Well they all are, really, aren't they? Girls and women. In this together.

7

• • • • • • •

Luckily for me, when the bill comes Angelica insists on paying, so I allow her to talk me into going halves. Okay, this doesn't conform to the rules of DatingTips.com but there's no other way out. Anyway, Angelica seems in a hurry to leave the café a good half an hour before her bus is due. I don't know why. It's a bit nippy outside and we have to stand at the bus stop waiting, and I don't really see the point.

At least there's a shelter, which is handy because spots of rain appear. Angelica leans against the smeared, graffiti-splashed plexiglass of the bus shelter with her arms folded. We talk a bit about Matt and Tonga and about them seeing us out together. I mention that I was amazed they were so childish. She says they weren't too bad. I say I was *very* amazed that they were so childish. So childish.

Then Angelica shivers. She takes a tiny step towards me. 'I'm cold,' she says, hugging herself.

'Yeh. We should have stayed in the café a bit longer.'

Then she takes another step towards me and goes, 'Brrrrrrrrrrrrrrrrr.'

'Yeh. 'Tis a case of brrrrrrrrrrrr, innit?'

Then she looks at me intently and makes a little swing of her shoulder.

'What?' I say.

Then she swings her shoulder again, just a fraction. This girl is completely weird. I mean you don't need a long, coiled, forked tongue to be weird, do you? All you need to do is make these unfathomable little movements.

'Wish I could get warm,' she says.

I wonder if perhaps she's cold-blooded, or something like that. That would fit in with the reptile thing. 'Do you want to go back to the café for ten minutes?'

'Oh for God's sake!'

'What?'

Then she goes all kind of gooey-eyed, and in a quiet voice she says, 'Warm me up.'

This has me scratching my head. I don't mean I actually reach up and shake the old dandruff free; I mean it has me baffled. I do think that if a girl wants someone to warm her up then she should just say so. Talking about the weather and swinging the shoulders and making all these little shivers and shudders doesn't really help a bloke, does it? Why not just come out with it? I certainly don't object to a cuddle. Not going to say no, am I, and I'm not the sort of person who needs telling twice.

I step closer and give her a hug.

'Not too tight,' she says.

Not too tight! What's a bloke supposed to make of that? Well, I'm still wondering where that leaves me when she comes in close and gives me that gooey-eyed soulful look again. I think she can do it to order. Probably all girls can. I bet they practise it at home in the mirror.

It's probably quite useful. Rather than say outright *I'd like to snog now*, it gives them a clever way out. In case they change their minds at the last minute.

I kiss her, and it's good. I like the taste of her lips. I can taste the ice-cream. There's no garlic or onions or strong cheese; not a hint of anything like that. I'm kissing her wondering if she can taste the coffee I had. At least that's not too bad. I know I've got a fibre of beef stuck between my teeth from lunchtime. I brushed my teeth before coming out this evening but I couldn't quite get to this one fibre. I expect it's rotting away there, but I'm trying not to think about it.

We press our lips together pretty hard and keep at it for quite a while. You don't want to break off too early. If you break off too early it's like saying you don't like someone, or maybe you're saying that their mouth reeks of rotting meat. They didn't go into it on DatingTips.com. They didn't actually say how long a first kiss should last. They've missed a trick there. I might email them and suggest it as an area they might cover. Or I might set up my own website for dating tips. I'd be very clear about these things. I would say not less than three minutes but not more than four minutes because you need to come up for air eventually. And also you might need to look around to see if anyone else has turned up at the bus stop. They might be standing just behind you.

• • • •

We go on kissing and I'm not sure how long it's been. You can't just look at your watch and then carry on, because that's just like breaking off. I suppose you have to guess three minutes give or take ten seconds. There's no other way.

Just when I think the three minutes is up she tries to poke her tongue between my lips. This comes as a bit of a shock because I'm not quite ready for it. Anyway, I press my lips together a bit harder because that thing about her tongue is still bothering me. What if she does have a lizard tongue after all? What if she uses it to reach deep down inside you, like halfway down your throat. Maybe to plant alien seeds in your digestive system. It's not so crazy.

I try to edge back from her, but she just presses harder towards me, even though we're now well past the required three minutes. She puts her tongue on my lips. Then I think I'm being stupid, but I'm not going to let her just shove it in my mouth without checking, so I use the tip of my own tongue to touch the tip of her tongue, just so's I can feel the shape of it. I want to be sure, that's all.

It feels normal enough. Slippery and soft and wet. We touch tongues and she giggles.

I do it again. I can't feel any fork shape there, so I let her tongue come inside my mouth a bit more. She giggles again.

I pull back. 'What is it?'

'I dunno. You're a funny kisser.'

'Oh! Pardon me!'

'No! A nice kisser.' And then she squeezes up to me again so that we can go another round. I don't mind it. I think it's probably okay if she comes in a bit further with her tongue, though I wish I could get rid of the idea that it's going to unwind about three feet and either go up my sinuses and grab my brain or down the throat and start mucking about with my organs. So I just let it in a bit.

Luckily before I have to let it all the way in we hear the big diesel engine of the bus drawing up. We stop kissing and she jumps out of the shelter waving at the driver. He spots her in time and stops the bus.

I see her safely on to the bus and then I turn and walk

towards my own bus stop. Before I get chance to cross the road her bus starts up again, comes juddering alongside me and stops quickly as the traffic lights turn red. Angelica has taken a window seat but she hasn't seen me. I'm just about to tap on the window to wave a cheery farewell when a weird thing happens.

Angelica has a small tissue in her hand and she's wiping make-up from her face. Then through the misted glass of the bus window I see Angelica reach up to prise open her left eye with a thumb and forefinger. She opens her eyelid and her eyeball plops into her hand. I'm close enough to the bus to see the eyeball glow metallic red and gold, like it's made up of moving microcircuits.

It's so scary my heart crashes in my chest. For a few seconds I can't breathe. Then the traffic lights change and the bus moves off again. I watch it turn the corner at the traffic lights. I'm left staring after the bus like an idiot, with my mouth hanging open.

And then the rain comes down on me. Really heavy rain.

•••••••

'Oooh, our Doogie,' my mum says when I get in. 'You look like a drowned rat.'

There was no shelter at my bus stop and the bus was late so I got soaked. That's what gets me about people who organise these things. How come at Angelica's bus stop there's a shelter then across the road there isn't one? What's the sense in that? Do they think it's only going to rain in one place?

'Are you all right, our Doogie? You don't look very well. Does he, Dad?'

Dad was sitting in the kitchen sorting out his fishing tackle. Once he kept a tin of live maggots in the fridge. It's the only time I've ever seen my mum go mad. 'He looks like he needs a good wash.'

It's what he always says. I could come home with an axe embedded in my skull and he'd say I look like I need a good wash.

'Shall I run you a hot bath, our Doogie?'

'Yeh,' I say weakly. Not because I agree with my dad about needing a wash, but because I feel a bit weird. About Angelica I mean, and what happened. First there was that business with the lizard tongue. Then I convinced myself that it was just my mind playing tricks. Now I've seen her pluck a cyborg eye out of her face.

It's not funny any more.

I need to tell someone about this, and soon. I don't know what is going on but it gives me a bad feeling. I've no idea where to start. Maybe I should go to the police station, but somehow I just know I won't be taken seriously. I don't even think about telling Mum or Dad. Firstly, I haven't even mentioned anything about having a girlfriend. Then if I do say anything I'm going to have to tell them she's probably called Xt'Qpppllz and she comes from sector nine of the fourth quadrant. *'Oh that's nice, our Doogie, shall we have her round for tea and a slice of Battenberg cake?'*

No. No, no, no.

I get out of the bath, get dried and get into my jimmies. I go down and tell Mum and Dad that I'm going to bed early. Mum looks concerned, Dad looks up from tying his hooks. If anything he looks suspicious. 'Night, son,' he says.

In my room I power up my computer and log on to the Internet. I make another search. This time I put the words *lizard tongue*, *eyeball* and *alien* into the word-search. You wouldn't think those words could pull up so much porn but they do. Anyway after sifting (why do they call it surfing – as if wading waist deep through the decomposing garbage found in the heads of psychos, religious nuts, demon-worshippers and porno-merchants is anything like surfing on a beach? Well I've been to Newquay with my surfboard on a hot summer's day. I don't think one thing is much like the other) I finally come across a message board. And the people are talking about whether or not we might have aliens living amongst us.

Everyone on the message board seems very polite, reasonable and well mannered. No trolls, no flamers, no screamers, no shouters. No one seems to be saying yes, no one is saying no. They all seem to agree that it might well be the case.

There's also a live chatroom. I quickly register with the screen-name of Thunderthighs. (I don't know why, it just popped into my head and I didn't want to register my real name.) Anyway, I lurk in the chatroom, not joining in, just following the discussion.

There are about a dozen people in the chatroom and to be truthful, they're not saying much. The talk isn't even about aliens at all. It's all that *how ya doing?* type of stuff. Someone called Filmflam had an operation on his knee and is going on an on about it. Someone called Joo-Joo97 is moaning about how her in-laws drive her mad.

I decide to type in a general question for anyone in the room: *If you suspect someone is an alien, what are the first signs you look for?*

It's a weird thing but all the conversation stops, just like it might in a real room. The cursor blinks, but no one is saying anything any more. Even Joo-Joo97 has stopped slagging off the in-laws.

Then someone called Bladerunner969 types: *Tell us a bit about yourself, Thunderthighs.*

I start by saying a bit about where I'm from and I add on a few years and then after a few minutes I realise that everyone in the room thinks I'm a girl. Maybe because of the Thunderthighs thing. Well it's not a nice feeling. For one thing these guys are falling over themselves to talk. I get goosebumps up and down at the thought of this. Imagine going around being thought of as a girl. Nightmare.

I quickly put them right, and guess what? All these 'interested' guys go back to having their own conversations. What a bunch of creeps. One minute they're all like flies round a bull's arse, then they treat you like a fart in a lift. That's out of order. Personally in life I treat everyone as equal. I don't give a damn whether they are short, tall, black, white, male or female, it's all the same to me, and that's how it should be.

At last the guy called Bladerunner969 talks to me. He gives me an email address. He tells me to send a blank email with nothing written in the subject line and nothing in the box. I ask why and he says — and he's a bit rude if you ask me — that I should just do it.

I do exactly that while I'm still in the chatroom. Then I notice Bladerunner969 saying his goodbyes to everyone, and before he leaves he says that I should remember the number 24791. Then he's gone. Logged out.

After a few moments an email comes through to me from someone called smokeandmirrors@peshwari.com. We begin an email back and forth.

smokeandmirrors@peshwari.com: Is that Thunderthighs?

Me: Yes, who is that?

smokeandmirrors@peshwari.com: Don't use my name. Sign out from the chatroom.

Me: Okay.

I sign out of the chatroom. I guess this must be Bladerunner969 but I don't know what the hell is going on.

smokeandmirrors@peshwari.com: Good. Remember that number?

Me: Yes.

smokeandmirrors@peshwari.com: Good. Don't type it or

write it anywhere, just keep it in your head and take them there.

Me: Where?

smokeandmirrors@peshwari.com: There.

Me: Where?

smokeandmirrors@peshwari.com: I'm going to send you a weblink which will guide you to an Instant Message box. At first it will seem broken, but you'll figure it out.

Me: what's all this about?

smokeandmirrors@peshwari.com: Just a precaution. Don't worry. Bye.

• • ••

I wait for a while and nothing happens. It's late. I've been on the computer for quite a while. I go and brush my teeth and get ready for bed, but when I return there's still nothing. Then I hear Mum and Dad coming to bed.

Dad sticks his head round the door. 'Come on, matey, it's after eleven. Switch that thing off and get your head down.'

My computer is always 'that thing' as far as Dad is concerned. I do as he says and jump into bed. I lie in the dark but my head is spinning. Angelica. The eye. The tongue. Thunderthighs. Bladerunner969. Smokeandmirrors. 24791.

• • ••

I wake up in the morning with a start. I flick the computer switches and log on to my server. No email from Bladerunner969 or Smokeandmirrors, but there is a new email from Matt and some junk mail from an address with a scramble of numbers. Matt's reads: Oi, you shagging her then?

I write a one-word answer to Matt and send.

I go to dump the junk mail and then I have second thoughts, because buried in the email title is the sequence **24791** in bold, which is the number Bladerunner969 gave me. So I open up the email. There is a link. I click it and nothing happens. Sure enough it's broken, just as Bladerunner969 said it would be. I look at the link and in the middle of a scramble of letters and numbers the word THERE stands out in capital letters.

I remember that Bladerunner969 told me to take the numbers there. So I delete the word THERE and paste in the numbers. I hit the link and sure enough, this time it takes me to an Instant Messaging box. Someone called Van Helsing is waiting.

Van Helsing: Thought you'd never get here.

Me: What's all this about? Are you Bladerunner969? I'm Doogie, by the way.

Van Helsing: Yes. Don't use your real name again. Okay, I'm afraid I'm going to have to leave for work in a couple of minutes. We can use this box to talk. It's relatively safe.

Me: Are we being monitored?

Van Helsing: Probably not, but it's always possible. Sorry about all the espionage stuff, I know it seems silly. This is just a precaution we've all agreed on.

Me: Who is we?

Van Helsing: We're a small group.

Me: The chatroom people?

Van Helsing: No. At least not all of them. Look, you can contact me any time on the email address I gave you. Just don't mention you-know-what in the subject line. Put something boring in the subject line. Make out you're a geek.

Me: I am a geek. Bit of.

Van Helsing: Well, make out you're an even bigger geek.

Me: What for?

Van Helsing: I really have to go. But I'll be here this evening around six. That's if you want to talk about this thing. If not, no problem and goodbye.

The IM box tells me that Van Helsing has logged out.

I'm still staring at the monitor when I hear Mum. 'Doogie!! Our Doogie! Come and get your Breakfast Nutty Crunch or you'll be late for school, our Doogie!'

9

That day at school it's a bit of a relief to find that Angelica isn't there. I've no idea why not. She hasn't made any close friends among the other girls in class so there's no one to get information from. I wonder if she's reporting back. I'm not sure who she'd be reporting back to. I think about this all through Maths, and it makes me feel a bit sweaty.

Matt and Tonga of course have told a few hundred people that Angelica and I are going out. Shelly Hobbs asks me if it's true, and then before I have time to say yes or no or rub my arse she announces it to the whole class. I mean she actually puts her hands to her mouth to shape a megaphone. So that's it then.

When lunchtime comes round I eat in the school canteen.

'Did you get a feel?' says Tonga.

'No.'

Tonga shrugs.

'Did you get a snog?' Matt wants to know. His mouth is full of pizza. Crumbs are falling from his lips. He has tomato paste on his chin. I don't feel like talking about snogging.

'No,' I lie.

Matt shrugs.

Tonga shrugs back at Matt. Matt shrugs back at Tonga.

Shrug. Shrug. Shrug. Then they laugh, Matt shooting half of his mouthful of pizza across the table.

'Sod off,' I say.

'Touchy!' says Matt.

'You finished?' Tonga says to me, getting up. 'Let's play footie.'

I hang back, waiting until Matt and Tonga have gone. The doors from the school canteen open out on to the yard where we always kick a ball about, but there's a back door that runs by the science block, and I take that instead.

I'm going to see Pinky Lewis.

I don't know why, but Pinky Lewis our science teacher doesn't have his lunch with the rest of the staff. He has a plastic sandwich box and a thermos flask and he spends his lunchtimes alone, scoffing his sandwiches and reading from a magazine called *New Scientist*. We think this is because the other teachers think he's weird and won't let him sit with them in the staff room. Well, he is weird.

He's weird because sometimes he talks to himself in science lessons. I mean he mutters on about stuff and then suddenly seems to wake up, like he's surprised to find himself in front of a classroom full of kids. How did I get here, sort of thing. Who are all these children, sort of thing. When that happens he turns bright pink and starts all over again.

But Matt told me he'd heard that Pinky was once a government consultant on space travel and had written some papers. He was involved in making some satellite crash-land on Mars, but he kept having nervous breakdowns so they made him teach science to kids instead, probably as punishment. That's what Matt said anyway. But he is very bright. He once explained time travel to the class so that even I could understand it.

Well, not understand it. No one can, apparently.

I see Pinky in his classroom nibbling on his sandwiches, deeply absorbed in the *New Scientist*. I tap on the door. At first he looks up like someone has caught him doing something he shouldn't be doing. Then he peers over my shoulder.

Pinky doesn't say anything. Neither does he beckon me in, so I knock again. He just stares at me. I think he's hoping I'll go away, but I don't. I open the door.

He dabs either side of his mouth with the back of his hand. 'Douglas.'

'Hello.'

'What is it, Douglas?'

The thing is I want to find a way to ask him what he thinks about the idea that there might be aliens living amongst us. But I'm not going to come right out and say that. He would probably just send me away. So I have to find a way to lead up to it.

'What's in your sandwiches?'

'Eh? What?' He looks confused for a moment, then he opens up one of his sandwiches, as if he can't remember. 'Tuna and mayonnaise.'

'Right,' I say.

There's a horrible pause. 'Did you come here just to ask me about my lunch, Douglas?'

I have to think on my feet. 'No. I'm doing a scientific study. Finding out what people have in their sandwiches, and then trying to see what the average thing is. For example if I ask one hundred people what they have in their sandwiches, and say ten or twenty say tuna, and ten or twenty say ham –'

He interrupts me. 'Douglas, what the blithering hell are you on about?'

'Okay,' I say, getting to the point, 'I wanted to know if you think there might be life on other planets.'

Pinky sighs deeply. Then he puts down his magazine, spreads his legs and puts a hand on each knee. 'Has someone sent you here to pull my leg?'

'No! I want to know what you think.'

He squints at me and wrinkles his nose. The ginger hairs in his nostrils dance briefly. 'Well, Douglas, you can be pretty certain of it.'

'Really?'

'Look. We're living on a speck of dust in one galaxy. And that galaxy itself is a speck of dust in the universe.'

'I don't follow you.'

'In our galaxy alone there are about one hundred billion stars. And each of those stars has planets just like in our system. And there are countless galaxies in space. Not very likely that the accident of life has only happened on this one single speck of dust, is it?'

'No.'

'Of course we haven't much idea what form life would take elsewhere. It might be microscopic life. It might be gigantic.' And then I think he looks at me a bit strangely when he says, 'It might be intelligent and then again it might not.'

'Do you think they would visit this planet?'

'Who?'

'Other life-formitudes.'

'Aliens? Are you asking me about aliens?'

I nod.

'Only if they were extremely bored. Or perhaps on a long journey to somewhere more interesting. Like stopping for a sandwich at a motorway café.'

'But is it possible?'

'Anything is possible. It's possible you might one day pay attention to me in class. But is it likely? Less so. Why are you asking me these questions?'

'But are there people who think it has already happened?'

'Plenty of people. There are stories of folk being abducted by aliens. In the old days people used to tell tales of being abducted by fairies. Who knows, perhaps they are the same thing. Then there are people who think that visions of angels were really aliens in flying saucers. All sorts of daft ideas come along.'

Angels, I thought. Angelica. Funny. 'What would they want?'

'Who?'

'These aliens.'

'Well, I haven't said there are any!'

'No, but if they did come, what would they want?'

'Well, it would have to be pretty important. I mean they're not going to travel from one rim of the galaxy to the other just to get the latest Lily Allen CD, are they?'

'No.'

'No. It would have to be for vital resources. Minerals. Fuel. What have you.'

'Or perhaps they would want to harvest us human beings.'

'Harvest, Douglas?'

'Use our brains or whatever.'

'Yes. Perhaps they would find your brain interesting and

scoop it out and set it to work for them, these people with the blistering technology enabling them to travel from one rim of the universe to the other. Now I have one tuna sandwich left: do you think I might be left to eat it in peace?'

•• ●●

'Where did you get to?' Matt says.

'Flinnooforraba,' I say, waving an arm. It isn't anything. It's just a noise so they won't ask me any more questions.

'What's 'e say?' goes Wilko.

'Dunno,' says Tonga. 'Somethin' about his dinner.'

'Know what, Doogie?' Matt says. 'You've gone weird since you've been going out with the Inuit. Weird.'

'Inuit?' I say.

'What's an Inuit?' says Tonga.

'Eskimo. She looks like an Eskimo,' says Matt.

'Does she?' says Wilko. 'I wouldn't say that.'

'So what?' I chip in. 'You look like a twat but we don't go around saying Matt looks like a twat.'

'We do,' says Tonga.

'See?' says Matt. 'You make one remark about Eskimo Nell and he gets all fruity.'

'Fruity?' I say. 'What's fruity?'

'Fruity,' goes Tonga. 'Hahahaha. Fruity. Hahaha.'

'It's that girl,' Wilko adds for good measure. 'She's made you fruity.'

I leap at him and try to knuckle his skull, but he's too quick.

•• ●●

At home I finish my tea — pork sausage, mash and peas — real quick. Then I tell Mum I'm going up to my room to do some homework.

She looks at me like I've just said, *I love you, Mum*. Her eyes water a bit. 'Oh our Doogie. Hear that, Brian? Our Doogie is going to do his homework without being asked. Isn't that nice, eh, Dad?'

Dad's watching the box. Well, not really watching it. He's just staring at it with one eye closed and the other closing. He's the first to complain about the crap on TV but the last to turn it off. 'Eh?'

'Our Doogie,' Mom says.

'He's there,' Dad says, pointing a finger at me.

I shake my head. Mum makes that little gesture where she tucks her neck in and lifts up her shoulders. Dad waggles his finger in his ear wax and goes back to not watching the TV.

I'm early for Van Helsing. The chatroom is empty. I leave the window open and while away the time by playing Crack-whore on my PlayStation, which is quite a good game.

Bang on six I hear a gloop to announce that someone else has entered the chatroom.

Me: Hello. Is Van Helsing your real name?

Van Helsing: Of course not. I'm not giving you my real name.

Me: Oh.

Van Helsing: Don't worry. Just remember not to ask for it in future. Okay so why are you here, Holmwood?

Me: Holmwood?

Van Helsing: That's your new screen name for the purposes of this communication.

Me: It is?

Van Helsing: Yes. Now tell me why you're here.

I don't much like the idea of being Holmwood. I mean, what's that? Sounds like wormwood. I want to suggest a few other screen names. I have a few cool ideas, but it doesn't seem to be the time and place. Instead I just tell him everything about Angelica and what had happened; about the tongue, the super ability with languages, the high intelligence, the slightly weird looks and, finally, the android eyeball.

Me (I'm not going to call myself Holmwood; I'm just not. Obviously I type it in and it comes up on the screen but you'll have to imagine it.): Are you still there?

Van Helsing: I'm still here. Is that everything?

Me: Pretty much. *(I could tell him about DatingTips.com but it doesn't seem relevant.)*

Van Helsing: Well, it pretty much matches up to everyone else's experiences.

Me: It does?

Van Helsing: Generally, yes. I have to admit we have a couple of loonies in our group who see an extraterrestrial hiding behind every parked car. But discounting them, your experiences tally with the others. You see the tongue, then you don't. You see an odd facial feature, then you don't. They do have a fantastic ability with languages. And they look pretty much like us. How old are you?'

Me: Fifteen.

Van Helsing: Okay, you're old enough for me to ask you this. Has she shown any sexual interest?

Me: Eh?

Van Helsing: They seem to have a high interest in sex. Of course this is probably a cover so that they can get us in a position to do whatever it is they're after.

Me: What *are* they after?

Van Helsing: We don't know, Holmwood! That's the thing. They're here. They appear to be increasing in number. And we've no idea what they are up to or what they want from us. They appear to be biding their time.

Me: So what do we do? Shouldn't we go the police? Tell the government?

Van Helsing: Ha!

Me: Why is that not a good idea?

Van Helsing: Try it. When they stop laughing at you, they want to lock you up. All of our members have been through it. But don't let me stop you.

Me: How many are in this group?

Van Helsing: Over 200 members. But more like you are finding us every week. The extraterrestrials are here, Holmwood. It's a fact. But you'll get no help from the authorities. They just scoff. Don't even go there.

Me: But there must be something we can do!

Van Helsing: Oh there is. Plenty. Right now we're collecting as much information as we can. Addresses, information about their movements and actions. We're putting together a massive dossier, and when the time is right we'll all come out and present it to the media. But only when the time is right and when the evidence is inescapable.

Me: Evidence of aliens?

Van Helsing: We don't refer to them as aliens. Makes you think of little green men. They're much more sophisticated. We refer to them as extraterrestrials. They can easily look like people. They might even be part-human in origin. We just don't know yet. You want to help us?

Me: Errr . . .

Van Helsing: Up to you, Holmwood. You can be in or out. But you're in a terrific position. As far as we know, up until now no one has actually been harmed by them. But no one has been able to get a look inside the places where they're living. Their houses, their apartments. But if this girl is coming on to you, you have the perfect excuse. You invite her to meet the folks; then you get her to invite you back in return.

Me: Isn't that dangerous?

Van Helsing: Like I say. No one has been harmed. No, it's something else that they're after.

Me:

Van Helsing: You still there, Holmwood?

Me: Yeh.

Van Helsing: You want to play? You could be very important to us.

Me: Can I think about it?

Van Helsing: Sure. No pressure.

Me: Can you give me a phone number or something?

Van Helsing: It's important that we never meet each other. Never. We don't want them to connect up our membership. If they did that, they would know we are on to them. Look, I'll let you think about it. All you have to do is report back here, letting me know what you've found out. I'll be here every night at the same time. I'll wait five minutes. If you don't show up, no problem. But I'll keep checking. Okay, now I'm gone. Bye, Holmwood.

He leaves the chatroom. It just leaves me staring at the cursor blinking on the screen. I stare for a long time. After a while I log off the computer and power down. From downstairs I hear Mum and Dad laughing. If they knew what was going on I don't think they would find things quite so funny.

The next day Angelica is back at school. It's break time before she speaks to me. I'm leaning against the bike-shed wall, poking around in the corner of a bag of crisps when she comes over. Funny how she always has her arms folded when she comes over to me.

'Hi,' she says.

'Yeh,' I say. I don't know why. I meant to say hi but I say yeh. 'Hi.' And then I wink. I don't know why I wink. It's like it's more of a twitch of my eye than a real wink. Like a twitch that got converted into a wink. I don't know what's going on. As soon as she comes near, my mouth and my eye start behaving badly, doing things I didn't want them to do. I wonder if she's doing it.

'Did you miss me?' she says.

'Where were you yesterday?'

'I have a bit of a cold.'

'Oh. No more snogging for us then!' I say this a bit too quickly. I mean it's a relief, but it comes out like I'm a bit too keen not to snog.

She looks a bit hurt. 'You gave it to me, the other night!'

'Did I?'

'Yes, you did.'

'Sorry.'

She smiles. 'I don't mind.'

I suppose that's meant to be a compliment, but it makes me think of that film where the Martians invade and zap everyone with death rays until the common cold germ wipes them out. I hope my common cold germ isn't going to wipe her out. I do feel a little bit sorry for her if that's going to happen.

'I thought we could walk over Black Bank at lunchtime,' she suggests. 'Skip lunch, you know.'

Black Bank? Black Bank is an area of rough open ground either side of the canal, about a quarter of a mile from the school. When anyone says Black Bank they mean ciggies or snogging. And since neither Angelica nor I smoke ciggies it can only be for one thing.

'You're keen!' I say.

'Yes,' she says. And she winks at me. 'I am.'

I think she needs hosing down a bit. She's obviously mad for it. I act like I'm cool, but that thing starts happening again: all the blood in my body becomes like wet cement and my heart starts knocking. Truth is I'm a bit scared of her when she's like this, but I'd rather die than show it. 'Well,' I say, 'let's not skip lunch. I'm pretty hungry. He he. But we can nip up Black Bank after.'

Her face falls. I don't know what to say, but I don't have to say anything, because I'm saved by the bell signalling the end of break. Phew!

● ● ● ●

I have lunch with Tonga, Matt and Wilko, then I make myself a bit scarce afterwards. She finds me, looking a bit cross. 'There you are! We won't have time to go over Black Bank!'

'Oh, why didn't you say?'

'I did say! Where have you been?'

'I had to get something from the library.'

'Suddenly learned to read, have we? What's brought on this attack of intelligence?'

She's got a nasty tongue this girl, I think to myself. Then I think, yeh, of course she has. 'Okay then, let's go to Black Bank.'

'No,' she says airily. 'Too late. No point.'

I try not to let my mouth fall open. Then I suddenly remember something I read on DatingTips.com. Something that makes it all perfectly clear.

> Guys, watch out for what we at DatingTips.com call the 'super-swing'. So she presses you all day, or over several days, about wanting to do a particular thing, such as take you to meet her friends. You resist, but when you finally agree she claims to have lost interest and it's your fault. That's it. That's the 'super-swing' and you just got suckered. She merely wanted to see how far she could control you! When she hits you with the 'super-swing' there's only one way to respond: make out you don't give a rat's ass.

So it looks like I just got the super-swing treatment. Luckily for me, thanks to DatingTips.com, I know how to handle it.

I shrug. 'Who cares?' I say.

But she goes off like a rocket. I mean she nearly explodes. '*What?* What did you say?' Her eyes look wet again and she clamps her teeth together.

'Who cares about Black Bank, I mean,' I say quickly. 'I didn't mean that I don't care about you.'

'You've got a funny way of showing it!'

'I was just going to ask you to do something else.'

'Like what?'

'Err . . . come to my place. After school. For tea.'

She looks puzzled. She blinks and shakes her head. 'What? Meet your mum and dad, you mean?'

Well, now she says it, the thought does sound worse than being zapped by an alien death ray, but once again my mouth seems to take over and I hear myself saying, 'Yeh.'

'When?'

'Today. After school.'

'At your house? With your mum and dad?'

'My dad's a builder. It's not like they're going to suck your brains out, is it?' I wish I hadn't said that.

She blows out her cheeks. 'Well, I could phone my mum and tell her.'

'Right.'

Then she gives me a very strange look. Like I'm not to be trusted. 'I'll call her and let you know,' she says.

• • • •

I trail Angelica into the house behind me. Mum's hoovering. Dad will be home from work later. I think this is the best way. I figure I can work through them one at a time. Dealing with both my mum and dad together about anything can be a nightmare. The door slams behind us. Angelica is looking round the kitchen, taking it all in. I suddenly feel a bit embarrassed about the details. There is a pair of rubber gloves turned inside out on the work surface. A bottle of sauce is turned upside-down so my skinflint dad can get the last drop out of the bottle. Our kitchen clock has A Souvenir From Alton Towers plastered across its face. How naff can you get?

I hear the vacuum cleaner power down. 'Is that you, our Doogie?' Mum steps through from the lounge to the kitchen. She sees Angelica, and almost leaps back into the lounge with surprise. She claps her hands under her chin and rolls her eyes and tilts her head to one side. I mean it's my mother who starts to behave like an alien! 'Ooooooooo, our

Doogie! Who's this then? Our Doogie, you didn't tell me you were bringing a visitor!'

I try to pretend my mum doesn't exist.

'Hello, Mrs Townsend, I'm Angelica.'

My mum actually curtsies. Yeh! Curtsies! Yeh! Like the Queen just came in for a cup of tea and a jam tart. I'm not making it up! A curtsy! A little bob of the head and a bend of the knee. Jesssssssssssuuuuuuuussssssssss, get me out of here.

'Hello, petal, our Douglas is a one, isn't he? Didn't tell me anything about anyone coming! Just like his dad! All the same, men, aren't they, Angelica? Come into the lounge. I'll make all of us a nice cup of tea.'

'Steady on, Mum. What's this *all of us*? You don't have to make yourself one, you know. This isn't a tea-drinking convention. Don't feel pressured to join in.' Heck, I didn't even want tea myself.

'Doogie!' Angelica protests.

'Isn't he awful!' Mum goes. 'He's just pretending to be awful, petal. Take no notice.'

'No, Mum, I am being awful. That's me: awful. We haven't come round here to drink tea.'

'I'd love a cup of tea,' Angelica chimes in.

'What? You don't drink tea at the Café Vienna! You never drink tea. You're just saying it.'

'Oooh is that where you go, our Doogie? Lovely! I've always wanted to go in there, and, you know, hear the coffee geyser going off and on.'

I groan. Mum dances out to the kitchen. Now Angelica knows that the height of my mum's ambition is to listen to the espresso machine. Like it's opera.

'Calm down, Doogie! You're so rude to your mum.'

'No I'm not. My mum's lovely but she's so thick she doesn't know if anyone's being rude.'

'Doogie!'

• • • •

We sit down and Angelica glances about her, and I know she's taking it all in. 'Is that a bar?' she says.

'Yeh.'

My dad built a cocktail bar in the corner of the room as a surprise for my mum's birthday. When he unveiled it for her I could tell by the look on her face that she didn't think much of it, but she pretended to be pleased. When they have friends over my dad goes and stands behind it to serve drinks with little cocktail umbrellas in them. I mean, even if he has to go back into the kitchen to get something from the fridge he goes all the way back to the bar to serve it. Cringe.

'And look at that telly!'

It is pretty big. That's Dad again. Got to have the biggest. Right now it looks like a small spacecraft in the corner of the room. We have speaker towers dotted about the room, too, to get the surround-sound effect, but we can never get it to work properly.

'That's the biggest telly I've ever seen. It's massive! Massive!'

'All right! No need to go on and on about it!'

'I'm just saying it's huge.'

Mum comes in and I can't quite believe it but she's dusted off the 'hostess trolley'. It's basically a couple of trays on wheels and we never ever use it. My mum got it from her mum. Maybe it goes back several generations. Anyway, it sits in the kitchen, usually with junk on it. But Mum has moved the junk and in she wheels the bloody silly contraption, smiling like she just invented it, or like it's an heirloom. And guess what? Best china. I knew it. There's also a cake plate on a stand – how naff can you get? On the cake stand is a Battenberg cake with three slices already cut and a few ginger biscuits.

I knew it was a big mistake coming here.

Then Mum goes through the whole nightmare ritual: does Angelica like her tea strong? Does she have milk? Does she take sugar? I feel like hiding behind the sofa until they get all this over with.

'He's very secretive, our Doogie, you know. He hasn't told me a word about you!'

For God's sake! We had a cup of coffee together! It's not like we ran off and got married and had the police out looking for us and got our names in the papers, is it? Not like there's anything to tell, is it? Two people had coffee and then got on a bus, what's to tell?

'Well, I've only just started at this school,' Angelica says.

'Where were you before, petal?'

'We lived abroad.'

'Ah, that's lovely, Angelica. Hear that, our Doogie? Angelica lived abroad.'

'Yes yes yes.'

'Go and get your globe, Doogie.'

'What??'

She turns to Angelica. 'Doogie's got this lovely globe in his bedroom. It spins round. You plug it in and it lights up. Of course he's never used it. He had it for his birthday a few years ago. Never used it. But, look, Doogie, this is your chance.'

'Mum?'

'This is your chance to get your globe. So that Angelica can use it to show us where she's lived. Abroad.'

'I'm not getting it.'

'Go on, our Doogie.'

'No.'

'Listen to him, Angelica! Isn't he miserable!' Mum gets up out of her chair. 'I'll get it.'

'Oh leave it out, Mum!'

After Mum has gone, Angelica looks at me and raises her eyebrows. We don't say anything. Then Mum comes back with the globe. It's a crappy little thing. Mum sets it on the floor, plugs it in and it lights up. So does my mum's face.

'Thanks, Mum, you've just made me look like I'm seven years old.'

'Oh, isn't he sweet, Angelica! Oh.'

Then Mum sits back expectantly, waiting for Angelica to prod the globe. But something odd happens. Angelica looks slightly nervous, I think. Her previous confidence is lost for a moment. She's flustered. 'We've lived all over,' she says hastily.

'Show us then!' says Mum.

Angelica blushes. She gets up and jabs at the globe in about four different places. 'I'm not so great at geography,' she says.

Well, neither am I, but I'm a bit surprised to see her touch the middle of the Atlantic ocean. Like she was a fish or something. Okay, admittedly she did touch the globe a bit quick, but I'd swear I saw her finger brush the blue. 'Didn't you say you lived in Latria?' I ask her.

'Latria?' says Mum. 'Never heard of Latria.'

'Oh these states change their names all the time,' Angelica says. 'Dad says there's a revolution every two weeks and you have to learn a new name for the country. Can I use your toilet, Mrs Townsend?'

'Of course you can, petal. Upstairs and first on the left.'

Great, I think. Now she's also going to see the Spanish doll toilet-roll holder.

She skips upstairs and Mum retracts her neck and narrows her eyes at me. She mouths a word at me. 'Lovely.' Then she pouts at me, and mouths at me again. 'So pretty, our Doogie.'

I swear I'm going to hurl.

'I'd better get your dad's tea ready,' says Mum. 'Ask Angelica if she wants to stay.'

Angelica is quite a long time upstairs. A suspiciously long time. I wonder if she's creeping about my room, checking on me, getting information. This is what girls do: I know all about it from DatingTips.com. On DatingTips.com it tells you what to do if you take a girl back to your flat. Not that I have a flat but it's the same thing. Apparently girls wait until they have a chance to see if you have porn magazines in your flat. They don't like it and if they find one this reduces your chances of getting another date. So DatingTips.com recommends that you take your porn magazines away from all the obvious places and put them where they won't be found. You shouldn't put them under the bed or between the mattress and the base of the bed because these are the first places that girls look for your porn. You should also get rid of any underpants because these are also off-putting even if they don't have skid-marks. Luckily I don't have any porn magazines or underpants lying around. I'm pretty tidy.

I sit in the lounge twiddling my thumbs, looking down at the stupid illuminated globe and trying to exercise my ears to get a clue as to what's keeping her. Then, finally, I hear the bathroom toilet flush. She comes down the stairs at exactly the same moment that my dad arrives home from work. He's got plaster dust in his hair and all over his face. In fact his face is powdered white.

'Hello,' he says, looking at Angelica, 'who's this then?'

'It's Angelica,' Mum sings from the kitchen, poking at a pizza with a big fork. 'Our Doogie's girl.'

I could grab that fork off my mum and stab her with it. Really, I could.

'I won't shake hands, sweetheart,' Dad says. 'Until after I've had a shower.'

'Dad doesn't always have that stuff on his face,' I somehow find it necessary to point out.

'I know that,' says Angelica.

Dad goes up to get his shower and Mum continues to prepare the meal. Angelica and I go back into the lounge.

'You were a long time in the toilet,' I tell her.

'What?'

'Find anything?'

'Huh?'

'Oh, and it's not my idea but Mum wants you to stay and have dinner.'

Me: She's here now.

Van Helsing: Right now, in your house?

Me: Yeh.

Van Helsing: What's she doing?

Me: She's washing her hands.

Van Helsing: Why?

Me: Just about to have dinner with my folks.

Van Helsing: Right. Watch her closely.

Me: Eh?

Van Helsing: Study her, but don't let her see. Look at what she eats and what she leaves on the plate. There's a pattern. Watch the way she eats. Whether she swallows her food whole or whether she chews it over and over. In particular watch if she takes anything out of her mouth. Try to be casual though. You mustn't let her know she's under scrutiny.

Me: What's this all for?

Van Helsing: Make a full report after. This is important information.

Me: I have to go now. I'm being called.

Van Helsing: Okay. Remain calm. Don't give the game away. Oh and by the way, Holmwood.

Me: What?

Van Helsing: We appreciate it. All of us. We're waiting for your report.

Me: Bye.

Well, I do watch her over dinner. We're having pizza and oven chips. Normally we'd have junk food, but Angelica's here so we're not. Angelica doesn't seem to have much of an appetite. She eats a few chips and nibbles at her giant slice of pizza. But she seems more concerned with checking to see if she has pizza crumbs on her lips than in eating. Maybe if she is an alien she's been coached to do all these things just as a girl would: you know, go to the toilet for a long time, check the crumbs on your lips. I've no idea what would happen in alien training.

'I'll have to be getting back soon,' she says after we do the tinned fruit and ice-cream.

'We'll run you back in the car,' Dad says. 'Where is it you live?'

'Have you been to Angelica's house, our Doogie?'

'No, Mum.'

'Perhaps Angelica will invite you for tea one night.'

Angelica looks nervous at the suggestion.

'That would be lovely wouldn't it?' says Mum.

● ● ● ●

I lie awake that evening wondering if I've got it all wrong. What if Angelica is perfectly normal after all? What if she's an ordinary human being, but with one or two weird things about her that she can't help? Then I think: no, I saw that tongue! No, I saw that eye! Plus she gets in a flap if you ask her where she was living last year! Plus she takes half an hour to go for a pee! Well, not half an hour, but a quarter. Well, not a quarter, but a heck of a long time when you think of what little is involved. Even for a girl.

Then I think about what my mum said, about her being pretty. Well she is if you look at her one way; but then she's not if you look at her another way. And anyway, if you were trying to pass yourself off as human, you're not going to make yourself the female Hunchback of Notre Dame, are you? It wouldn't work. So you'd have to be pretty, wouldn't you? Unless you made yourself exactly in the middle of beautiful and ugly. That way you'd probably be invisible. But that would be no good if your aim is to get a boy, stick your tongue down his throat and suck out his brains. Would it? I mean you've got to be good-looking enough to get a few fellahs. I mean, I'm not bad. I'd prob give myself a seven. Seven or eight or nine. Somewhere around that. So she'd have to be quite pretty to get hold of someone like me.

I fall asleep with these things whizzing around in my brain.

● ● ●●

Next day she returns the invitation. I mean at break time she tells me she's spoken to her folks and we can go back to her house after school. I say I will, but I spend the rest of the day trying to think of an excuse to back out. I mean, what if this is it? What if I end up in a silk cocoon, being used as a battery for some alien beings? What if they want to make experiments, look up my arse, all that stuff?

You hear about these things.

I remember seeing something on DatingTips.com. It said you should always get an address of wherever you're going and leave it with a friend. On DatingTips.com it said that you might have a date with some woman who wants to drug you and steal your wallet. Well, I don't have a wallet; if I have any cash it usually just gets folded up in the corner of my pocket. So if a woman does drug me she will have to look through all my pockets before finding anything.

Anyway I know the address from when we dropped her off last night. Still, I write it down and leave it in my locker at school. I think if the police or government agencies investigate my abduction they will probably go through my stuff at school. Then I have to go back to my locker because there's a titty magazine in there I wouldn't want anyone to see that I've got. The lock is broken on Matt's locker so I stick the magazine in there. Then after I've done that I compose a short note saying what will have happened to me, and telling them how to contact Van Helsing to explain everything.

'You are still coming, aren't you?' Angelica says to me at the end of the day.

'Yeh. Sure.'

'Only you seem a bit weird.'

'Weird?'

'Yeh. Distracted. Like you don't want to talk to me. Like you're not sure. Just say if it's not what you want to do.'

'You mean if I don't want to come back to your place? Or if I don't want to go out with you?'

'Any of it. Just say.'

'No, I'm fine with all of it.'

'Perhaps I should count myself lucky?'

'Huh?' I say.

'Forget it. Come on, we have a bus to catch.'

It all feels weird. I don't normally get this bus and all the other kids are looking at us, like: what's he doing on this bus? I hate that. A person gets on a bus they don't usually get on and everyone looks at you like you've got two heads. You should be allowed to go around getting whatever bus you like. Even if you want to go in the opposite direction; I mean, it's up to you, isn't it? It's your business, not theirs.

Angelica lives in a leafy, tree-lined street full of detached houses of different sizes. My dad told me that the people who live in this street are 'worth a bob or two'. I don't know what a bob is but I guess he must be right. They all seem to have Beamers and Mercs parked in the drive. Oh, except for Angelica's house. They have a pick-up truck. It has a sticker on the petrol cap saying *Warning: converted to biofuel*.

Maybe that's the answer to space travel. Prob not, but it's a thought.

Angelica lets us in with a key. It's a huge house but the hall is a mess. The walls are scuffed, the paintwork is chipped. There's a coat-rack with a broken peg. My dad would spend every spare minute fixing these things up. There are also piles of books on the stairs. I don't mean a few books, I mean hundreds. Luckily the stairs are massively wide so you could step through the piles of books on either side.

'Mum's out,' Angelica says, 'but my dad's in. He's working in his study. We won't disturb him.'

'He works from home?'

'Mostly. He's a software engineer.'

'What, he programmes computers?'

'Well it's a bit more than that. He's at the cutting edge. He's already working on the generation of computers you won't see for another three years. You want a drink?'

'Yeh. I'll have a Coke.'

'We don't have Coke or soda in the house. Sugar rush is bad for you.'

'It is?'

'Yeh. Plus it makes my dad go a bit wappy.'

'Coke makes him go wappy?'

'Me too. A bit.'

'What do you do? Run around biting people?'

She leans towards me and clacks her teeth, inches from my nose. It's a joke but I wish she hadn't done it. Then she says, 'We can go up to my bedroom if you like.'

'What, your folks won't mind?'

'Mind? Why would they mind?'

'My mum wouldn't let me take a girl up to my bedroom.'

'Why ever not?'

'She doesn't think it's proper.'

'Well no one minds here. Let's go up.'

I remember what Van Helsing told me, about them being mad for sex. It makes my skin flush. 'No, let's stay down here. For a bit.'

She wrinkles her nose at me. 'Okay. Shall I make a cup of tea?'

'Yeh. Great.'

She tells me to take a seat in the lounge. I do. The room is in just as much of a state as the hall, but now I see why there are so many books on the stairs. The wall is lined with book-cases on three sides. Books are groaning on every shelf. There are also piles of books and magazines on the floor, on the coffee table, everywhere. But something is bothering me about the room big-time.

Then it hits me. No telly.

I wonder what sort of people wouldn't have a telly.

Perhaps the flickering light hurts their eyes. Or maybe the TV signals coming into the house disrupt their brain patterns. I'm just guessing, but I think it would be something like that.

Angelica comes back in with the tea. No best china this time. It's a couple of chipped mugs. 'Oh I forgot. You take sugar don't you? No one takes sugar in this house but I'll see if we've got some.'

There's another thing. Now I'll readily admit that if you take these things on their own – no telly, no Coke, no sugar and so on – they don't mean anything at all. But added up, it's a pattern. Take them all together and they start to add up to evidence.

When Angelica comes back into the lounge she's carrying a little ceramic sugar bowl. The sugar in the bowl is yellow in parts and it looks like it's been there untouched for fifteen years. It's gone crusty and hard. There is even a dead ant in there. She gives me the spoon and shudders. 'I don't know how you can have that stuff in your tea.'

I look at the dead ant and think: no, I don't know either. 'Why no telly?' I ask.

'Oh, there is one somewhere, under these books. We're not much of a telly family.' She sweeps a few books aside and there, true to her word, is possibly the smallest television you've ever seen in your life. The screen is about the size of a paperback book. It's pathetic, and I say so.

'Yes, but pretty much everything that's on the telly is pathetic, so what difference does it make? You could have your own cinema but if everything it shows is junk then what's the point?'

I'm about to argue with her when a man appears in the

doorway. 'Oh, hi, Dad!' She leaps up to him and kisses him on his jaw. Then she flops back down on the sofa.

Her dad is a big lumbering bear of a man, about six-six, unshaven, unruly jet-black hair sticking up at odd angles. His spectacles have strong black frames and the glass in them is so thick it makes his eyes look a long way away, like tadpoles swimming in spiral motion in a gluey pond. 'A-ha!' he says. 'A-hah!'

'This is Doogie,' Angelica says.

'A-ha!' he says again. 'So you're the Doogie!'

'Not the Doogie,' she says, 'just Doogie.'

'A-ha! Not the Doogie. A Doogie. Well I'm the dad. Not a dad. The dad.'

I look confused. Wouldn't you? 'Hello,' I say. 'How are you?'

The dad rubs his chin and looks at me thoughtfully. Then he remembers something. 'A-ha! Very pleased to meet you. Yes, I am. Very. Is that enough?' he asks Angelica.

'Well, you could ask Doogie a few questions like *how is school?* and things, but that's probably basically enough.'

'Oh, how is school, Doogie?'

'Fine,' I say.

'Now you just say *good* or some such thing,' she tells her dad, 'and then you can go.'

'Good. I can go back to work now?'

'Yep,' says Angelica, smiling up at him.

He lumbers off. I think he's gone but then he comes back. 'Doogie, I forgot to say nice meeting you. I always forget that part.'

'You too,' I say. 'Nice meeting you too.'

He nods, satisfied. Then he's gone again. Then he's back

again, but this time he gives me a little wave before leaving us for a third time.

'Yes, he's odd,' Angelica says. 'You can say he's odd. I don't mind.'

'No he's not odd at all,' I tell her. 'Well, not much. Well, quite odd.'

'Yes. He has Asperger's Syndrome. Know what that is? But he's very clever. I just have to teach him things, or remind him of things.'

'What like?'

'Well, he forgets to say *hello, how are you?* and *goodbye* and all of that. It's like he can't be bothered. It's not that he doesn't care. He does care. But he won't say *how are you?* if he doesn't really want an answer, like we do.'

I think about that a bit. I try to remember the last time I said *how are you?* Then I remember that it was about three minutes ago, to her dad. I mean, I wasn't saying *how are you?*: I didn't want him to tell me if he had a sore throat or what sort of a day he was having. I just meant: *how are you?*

'Where has he gone now?'

'Back to his office. Like I told you, he works from home. He really is a computer wizard, you know.'

'Wow!'

'But don't ask him to talk about what he does.'

'Why not? Doesn't he like talking about it?'

'The opposite. He'll tell you in minute detail. You won't understand a single word of it but that won't stop him. Are you sure you don't want to come up to my room?'

'No, I'm fine. Fine here. Drinking my tea.' I lift my cup to my mouth and take a slurp just to show her. It's too hot. I burn my lip. But I'm not about to give her an excuse to get me up there just so's she can suck my brains out.

No fear. I've seen enough. More than enough. I'm already eager to make my report to Van Helsing.

Angelica smiles at me. 'Is your tea okay?'

'Yes,' I tell her. 'But pretty soon I'll have to get my bus.'

11

●●●●●●●

Van Helsing: You'll have to go back.

Me: You must be joking! It's obvious what they are!

Van Helsing: You didn't get enough evidence. You made a run for it just as it was getting interesting.

Me: I didn't run! I finished my tea and let her walk me to the bus stop.

Van Helsing: Just as you were getting close to finding something out. I have to say, Holmwood, we're all a bit disappointed. You are the only one of us who has ever got inside one of their homes. There were a lot of people rooting for you.

Me: How many are there in your group?

Van Helsing: Never mind all that. Are you going to go back or not?

Me: You don't know what it's like! You should see her dad. He's massive and has a funny way of breathing. She has to teach him how to be a human being. How to say hello and all that. She pretended he'd got some condition or other . . . asp . . . asp . . .

Van Helsing: Asperger's Syndrome. Yes, that's their get-out-of-jail-free card. Whenever they do anything that alerts attention to the fact that they're not one of us they call it Asperger's Syndrome.

Me: Is there such a thing?

Van Helsing: Yes. Did he count your buttons?

Me: What?

Van Helsing: People with real Asperger's Syndrome want to count your buttons, or talk about lawnmowers. Don't be fooled. Do you think you can get inside her house again? You need to take a look at what he's working on with that so-called software.

I thought about it. I was doubtful if Angelica would even want to invite me back again. When she walked to the bus stop with me she seemed a bit put out that I had left so soon. She said she was waiting for her mum to come home and cook my dinner. Or cook me for dinner. No, I don't mean that, but it put me off. If Angelica's mum looked anything like her dad I didn't really want to meet her.

Van Helsing: You still there?

Me: I'm here.

Van Helsing: If it's all too much for you, say so, Holmwood.

Me: No. I'm all right with it.

Van Helsing: Sure?

Me: Yeh.

Van Helsing: Then set up another visit. Report back to me. We all believe in you, Holmwood.

Me: Right. Thanks.

Van Helsing: I'm gone.

● ● ● ●

'You run hot and cold,' Angelica told me at school, at break time.

'You're slow,' she told me at lunchtime.

'You're fickle and I never know where I am with you,' she told me at home time.

'Wait,' I said. 'Why are you getting at me all the time? What have I done to deserve this?'

'Do I really have to tell you?'

'Yes.'

'Right. Black Bank. Meet me at the rec ground there at seven. Maybe I'll tell you a few home truths about yourself.'

I go home on the bus, staring out of the window, trying to guess what those home truths might be. I have to ignore Matt and Tonga laughing, fooling around and ruffling my hair every five minutes. Tonga is showing off to Nina Scundy of Year Ten, she of the shining hair like a golden curtain, who often sits on the back seat, gazing at them with adoration. Then for nothing, and I mean nothing, Tonga slaps my ear pretty hard.

I grab his wrist and twist it behind him. 'Give over, Tonga.'

'Gerroff me, ya prat!'

'Give over then, will ya?'

'Gerroff me, ya prat.'

'Said give over, didn't I, you fat bastard?'

'Ow! Yer breakin' my arm!'

'Hey, leave him Doogie,' says Matt.

I let Tonga go. He's red in the face, nursing his wrist. I tell Matt, 'I'll do you too if you don't knock it off.' I mean it, and he knows it.

'What's got into you?' Matt says. 'You're no fun any more, Doogie. No fun.'

I look up and I see golden-haired Nina Scundy gazing at me, embarrassed by this little fracas. I get up and move to a different seat, up nearer the driver. They can bog off, cos they're bang out of order.

• • • •

The rec at Black Bank is a kids' playground, except that you don't get many kids there after six o'clock of an evening. I get there bang on seven but she's already there. It's a little chilly. I should have put a pullover on but I thought it would look cooler to go out in a shirt. So now I am cool. Freezing more like.

Angelica is perched on the slowly moving roundabout, her legs crossed at the ankles. Unlike me she has a coat on, a corduroy thing with a big belt. She's also wearing a black cap with a peak, maybe a Greek fisherman's hat. She's wearing a bit of lipstick and eyeshadow. She's painted her fingernails flamingo pink. She looks great. But sad.

I walk up to the roundabout and smile at her as she comes round. She doesn't return my smile. Round she goes, and I'm left looking at her back. The roundabout thing is only moving slowly, and it has a slight squeak to it as it goes, but it doesn't look like it wants to come to a stop. She comes round again. I smile at her again. She still doesn't smile back as, slowly, round she goes once more.

When she comes round a third time I give her the snarly face instead of a smile. Normally that sort of thing would make her laugh, but not this evening. The roundabout takes her away from me again and I wonder how long we can keep this up. This time I have no expression on my face. I'm a blank. So is she.

Now this is funny. Not funny ha-ha but funny peculiar. I mean this roundabout *has* to come to a stop some time. Otherwise it's a perpetual motion machine, and our physics teacher told us there was no such thing and never could be. But at the moment either I have to put my hand out and stop it, or Angelica could stop it by just putting out a foot.

Now I could stop it, but I'm remembering a line from DatingTips.com. It was offered under the heading: *what to do if you think you're about to be dumped.* Because I'm not stupid. I know Angelica has brought me here to dump me. That's why she's kind of dressed up. I read about all this on DatingTips.com.

> If your girl is about to dump you, rest assured that she will dress up for the occasion. The female of the species is hooked on high drama, and the only way she wants to go out of your story is in style. In fact if she surprises you by turning up in full battle-dress and make-up when you're least expecting it, you're about to bite the dust. When she says 'so long sucker', she wants you to see her walking out at her best.

Now if that were me and about to dump someone, I would do the opposite, just like any male would. I'd maybe eat a load of garlic and blue cheese so that my breath stank, pull on a pair of grease-spotted mechanic's overalls, rub some dirt on my face: that sort of thing. Then these girls wouldn't care much about what they were losing. But apparently girls just don't work that way.

> Okay, so she's dumping you. What can you do? Rage, scream, shout, sob? Go ahead. It will only make you look more of a worm in her eyes. So here's the way to go. Tell her it's all for the best. You heard me! Look hurt, then thoughtful and then give her THREE strong reasons why this is all for the best and number three reason is that you've been tempted by someone else but so far you've managed to resist but you didn't think

you'd be able to hold out much longer. Then sit back and watch the fireworks.

DatingTips.com says if you say this they go ape and the next thing is they demand to know who it is and then they say they've changed their mind about dumping you. It tells you not to reveal who that special person is – the one you can't keep your mitts off. Though I expect for most blokes, like me, it would be nobody.

Anyway, with this roundabout going round and around in its slow, squeaky little way I'm just wondering whether it would look like I care too much if I put out a hand when around it comes for about the ninth time.

'Aren't you cold in that thin shirt?'

I'm shivering. I have my hands dug in my pockets for warmth. I'm sure my nose is blue. 'No. Not at all.'

She reaches out a toe and stops the roundabout. I take it as my cue to sit next to her. As soon as I park my bum next to hers she touches the ground again with her toe and gets it moving again. Slowly.

We don't talk. I can see the backyards of the houses of the estate. One garden is beautifully maintained with flowers, another is a filthy bone-yard. Then I see the rusting hulk of a car at the corner of the rec where some joyriders have dumped and flamed it. Then there is the road and the dark woods behind it. Then the houses again.

I'm still shivering, and this is how we go, in silence: flowers, bone-yard, burned-out car, woods. Flowers, bone-yard, burned-out car, woods. Flowers, bone-yard, burned-out car, woods. And when we go past for the third time in silence I think: bugger this going out with girls thing, I'm going home.

I stop the roundabout and get off. 'You brought me here to dump me,' I say, 'so get on with it.'

She gasps.

'Admit it,' I say.

'Well . . .'

I was right. Or rather DatingTips.com was right.

'How did you know? Never mind. Here's three reasons why I think we should stop seeing each other —'

'What? No, *I* get to do the three reasons,' I say.

'Huh?'

'Sorry. Carry on. This should be interesting.'

'One, I don't think you care enough about me; two you don't even want to kiss me; three you don't seem to even like me.'

'Well,' I say, nodding my head. 'Firstly you'd have more time to do your homework, secondly you're too pretty, thirdly Nina Scundy.'

'What? What the hell are you talking about?'

I turn my back to her and pretend to be looking deep into the woods. That did not come out right at all. In fact that was crap. And I wasn't even supposed to mention Nina Scundy. In fact her name just popped into my mouth. Anyway, it seems to do the trick.

'Look, Doogie, I don't want us to finish but I wish you'd stop blowing hot and cold. One minute it's like you really do like to be with me; then the next thing is you're looking at me like I'm something from —'

'Outer space?'

She narrows her eyes and shakes her head. 'Why do you say that?'

'I thought that was what you were about to say.'

'No, I was going to say something from under a stone. Anyway the point is the same. How am I supposed to know what your feelings are towards me?'

'Why do you need to know that?'

She grabs her head in her hands and shrieks. 'Oh God!' It echoes all over the rec.

'Look,' I protest, 'I just don't go in for all that lovey-dovey stuff, okay?'

'I don't want lovey-dovey stuff, you perv! That's not what I'm saying.'

'Well, what *are* you saying?'

In exasperation she pulls the peak of her cap over her eyes and folds her arms. I think she's upset with me now. I get back on the roundabout beside her, but she won't let me look at her. Her eyes are damp, but she's making a good job of hiding it from me.

I look at her in her cap and coat and bell-bottom jeans, her dark hair cascading over her face and I feel really bad for messing her around, for hurting her. I want to put my arm around her but I'm not sure how she'll react. 'Angelica, what do you want me to do?' I ask her.

She looks up at last. She sniffs and thumbs back a tear. 'I want you to kiss me, dammit!' she says.

I look at the small rosebud of her lips and I think that's exactly what I want to do right now. It's no hardship. I put my arm around her and I breathe in her scent and I kiss her. Properly. I don't even care if she's going to bite off my tongue. My foot kicks out in a little spasm of pleasure and it sets off the roundabout again. I know we're turning but this time I don't see anything, because I have my eyes closed, and still kissing we go round and round and round.

12

....

Van Helsing: Be careful. It seems to me you're becoming emotionally involved with this girl.

Me: No way! I don't get emotionally involved with girls. They're fun to kiss or to try to get a feel. But that's where I draw the line, matey.

Van Helsing: You sure about that?

Me: Too bloody right. No way I'm going to waste my Saturdays.

Van Helsing: Okay. So long as you know the risks.

Me: Sure. (*What's he on about? I think. Does he mean the risks of getting involved with girls? Or the risks of getting involved with girls who are aliens?*) No problem.

Van Helsing: They have a way of tricking you into thinking they are human beings.

Me: What, girls?

Van Helsing: *(long pause here)* No, aliens.

Me: Right. That's what I meant.

Van Helsing: Keep your eye on the ball, Holmwood.

Me: Right.

Van Helsing: We want you to get in there if you can and take a look at the alpha male's office.

Me: The alpha male?

Van Helsing: The one she described as her father. He's not really her father. He's the one controlling the technology. If you can take a look at what's happening in that so-called home office of his, maybe have a look at the computers, it might give us a clue as to what they are up to.

Me: How do you know he's not her father? I mean, even aliens have fathers don't they?

Van Helsing: *(pause)* It's complicated. They don't reproduce like we do. They have hives.

Me: Hives?

Van Helsing: Like bees. They exist in cell-groups. They're just imitating family units so as to go unnoticed.

Me: I have another question, Van Helsing.

Van Helsing: Shoot.

Me: Well, what if these aliens just want to be like us and live like us, and be with us. What if they don't mean any harm?

Van Helsing: Holmwood, I don't mean to be rude but are you seriously suggesting these beings have travelled light years just to settle quietly on a planet that is in the grip of global warming, running out of water and natural resources, polluted, over-populated, heading at breakneck speed towards self-annihilation? Is that what you think, Holmwood?

Me: Well, no.

Van Helsing: This is the danger – you're allowing yourself to become emotionally involved with this female. This is how it happens. This is the thin end of the wedge. The slippery slope. I might have to pull you out of this mission if you can't hack it, Holmwood.

Me: What mission?

Van Helsing: Of going back to that house and collecting whatever information you can find.

Me: Right.

Van Helsing: Your mission, Holmwood. Your choice. No one is putting pressure on you here. Maybe it's unfair of us to ask these things of you. Just say the word and you're out. No harm done.

Me: No, I'm okay with it.

Van Helsing: You're a star. Now I'm gone. Talk tomorrow.

• • • •

Well, I get a chance to go back to Angelica's house when at school she tells me how disappointed her mum was that I didn't stay long enough to meet her. So I agree to go along a second time after school one night. This time I'm to stay for tea. I tell Van Helsing what I'm doing and I make sure he has the address of where I'm going. I'm to contact him by eleven o'clock on the night of my visit, so that I can report on anything I might have found out, plus to let him know that I'm safe.

'Getting serious, isn't it, our Doogie?' Mum is cutting me a slice of Battenberg cake after tea. 'Seeing a lot of her.'

'Just be careful it doesn't distract you from your school work,' Dad says, slurping from his tea cup.

'Eh?' I say. 'What you on about?'

'Can't be a scholar and a lover boy, can you now?'

'Leave him,' Mum says. 'I'm just saying don't get too serious.'

'I'm not serious!'

'Look at him!' Dad guffaws, spluttering Battenberg cake. 'He's red in the face! Ooh ya!'

'Who needs fathers?' I say. 'We should have hives instead.'

They both look a bit blank at this. Well, my mum and dad are a bit thick. Mum swallows her cake and says, 'Seeing a lot of each other though, eh, our Doogie?'

'Not really.'

'Can't be a scholar and spend all your time kissing and cuddling.' Dad again.

What's with this scholar thing? 'You what? I'm not listening to this.'

'Leave him alone. Just don't get too involved, eh, our Doogie. Because one thing leads to another, doesn't it, our Dad?'

'Eh? Oh, ah, oo, yes it do. Too bloody true.'

'And then before you know where you are, you're, well, you're where you don't want to be, aren't you , our Dad?'

'Oooh ya!'

It suddenly dawns on me that this is my mum and dad's idea of talking to me about sex. All this yada yada about one thing leading to another and then where would you be. I imagine them cooking up this conversation. No wonder my mum was pregnant with me when she was only eighteen if this is what she thinks passes for sex education. I feel sorry for them. I feel like putting my arm around my mum and saying it's okay, Mum, they give us condoms at school these days. Okay, they don't really give us condoms at school; but I feel like saying it.

Well, their idea of sex education is crap. 'Too right,' I say back to Dad. 'Ooooh ya!'

My dad puts his cup of tea down and stares at me hard. 'Are you taking the mickey?' he says.

'He's not, are you, our Doogie?' Mum says. 'He's not.'

'No,' I say. 'I'm just saying one thing doesn't lead to another. Not always. Not all the time.'

'What thing doesn't lead to another?' Dad asks me, sounding cross.

'Anything,' I say.

'He's just saying,' Mum says.

'But *what* is he just saying?' Dad says. There are yellow and pink crumbs of Battenberg cake sticking to his lips. He's getting more and more riled, but I can tell he doesn't even know what he's getting riled about.

'I'm just saying what I'm saying,' I say. Then I get out of my chair and go upstairs, because my dad is not beyond slapping my ear when he gets riled.

As I leap upstairs to my room I hear him say, 'Hear that? Bloody teenagers. He gets bloody worse.'

'You encourage him,' Mum says.

13

. . . .

I go home with Angelica after school the next day, and this time I get to meet the mother. Cripes! If there was any doubt in my mind about whether these lot are from another planet now all bets are off.

Firstly she's tiny. Secondly she's got this long, long red hair that comes way down and I mean way down, like she could sit on it and still have a spare handful. Her pale face is an explosion of freckles, like cinnamon sprinkled on rice pudding. What's more, she's wearing specs with bright blue plastic frames, but get this – there's no glass in the frames! I mean I'm dying to say why isn't there any glass in your specs, but I can't ask, because I know she's wearing them to pretend to be short-sighted and if I ask her then she'll know I've seen through her disguise and that I know she's only pretending to be a short-sighted human being.

Just like with her dad, there's no hello or how's it hanging or any of that. No, straight into a load of rubbish. 'Oooh,' she goes, 'he's good-looking, where did you find him then?' And then she smirks at me. And pulls a goofy face.

'Mum,' says Angelica.

'I'll say no more!' says her mum. 'Nothing. Nada. Rien. Does he drink tea?'

'He's got a name and he speaks,' says Angelica.

'Well no one's told me his name,' she snaps, 'and I haven't heard him speak.'

'I've told you his name several times!' Angelica protests.

Angelica's mum suddenly puts her fingers to her lips, shushing us. Then she clasps her hands together like someone praying and closes her eyes. After a few moments she suddenly shouts, 'DOOGIE! That's right, IT'S DOOGIE! I remembered! Look, Doogie,' she says to me, 'I may be an old bat but what a memory!!'

'Mum can tell you the value of pi to three hundred places, but she often can't remember what her friends' names are. So she gets excited when she does.'

'I see,' I say, not really seeing anything.

'He does speak! The Doogie does speak! Let's give him tea to excite his larynx some more!'

Out of his office comes Angelica's dad – or the alpha male as Van Helsing calls him – lumbering like a bear. 'What's all the shouting about?' he wants to know.

'It's Angelica. She's brought home a Doogie.'

'A what?'

She offers the palms of her hands towards me, as if making a presentation of me. 'A Doogie!'

He looks baffled. He takes off his own glasses – which do have glass lenses in them, that thick cloudy bottle-glass – and looks at me hard. 'That's Angelica's boyfriend!'

'I know that, you great big spiggit!' says Angelica's mum. 'His name is Doogie!'

Angelica rolls her eyes at me, while I wonder what a spiggit might be.

'Oh yes, we went through all that the other day,' he says,

rubbing his chin thoughtfully. 'And let me say this: how are you?'

'Very well, thanks,' I say, pleased to be able to say something in all this madness. 'How are you?'

He seems surprised by the question. 'Me? Well actually I'm good, too. I'm good because I'm working on a new idea which involves the complex sifting of binary chains —'

'He doesn't want to know that, Dad,' Angelica says.

'Of course not,' he says. 'I'm being a spiggit, aren't I?'

'You are!' says Angelica's mother, and they all laugh.

It's not that funny, but they all laugh a bit too long. I sort of laugh to join in with them. 'What's a spiggit?' I ask.

They all stop laughing and look at me.

The dad — the alpha male — scratches his chin. 'I don't really know. It's just something that Jennifer calls me. Jennifer, what is a spiggit?'

'Search me,' says Jennifer. 'It's just something I've been calling you for the past twelve years.'

'What?' I say. 'And you've no idea what it means?'

'She grins at me. 'No idea.'

'Shall we get a dictionary and look it up?' the alpha male asks.

'Don't worry about it, Dad,' Angelica says, grabbing my hand, 'we're going up to my bedroom.'

I'm a bit alarmed by this sudden initiative of Angelica's but to be honest I'm also relieved to get away from Jennifer and the alpha male. I follow Angelica and she leads me down the hall to the foot of the stairs. When I look back over my shoulder Jennifer and the alpha male are standing side by side making little coo-eey waving motions at me with their fingers. I mean it's not right. They seem a bit too pleased to see their daughter dragging a young bloke up to her room.

'I'll have dinner ready in an hour,' her mum says.

Then just as we are mounting the stairs the alpha male calls us back.

'I just remembered something,' he shouts.

'Duh?' I say, caught halfway up the stairs.

'School. How are things? At school. How are they?'

'Fine,' I say.

'Fine is good,' says Angelica's dad. 'Okay. Okay.'

When we get to her bedroom Angelica slams the door shut behind us. I do wonder if she is going to try to rip my jeans off, but she just slumps on the bed with her hands under her chin. 'Okay,' she says, 'they're *both* pretty weird, but they're my mum and dad and I love them.'

'Yeh.'

I look round the room for anything unusual. Equipment. Potions. Anything sinister. There is a computer workstation. On the wall is a poster of a boy band – the one where they all look like girls with soppy fringes and they're making signs with their fingers – actually they could be aliens. There's another poster of David Beckham and another pointless poster of a load of dogs. There are loads of beads and bangles hanging up, and silky scarves tied to the headboard of the bed, and some framed pictures of horses. I'm not sure if normal people would frame a picture of a horse or tie scarves to a bed.

'You're the first person I've brought home in years,' she says sadly.

'Oh?'

'I used to do it more when I was a kid and no one thought there was anything unusual. Then as they got older they started to notice. Look, Doogie, they're both really sweet-natured. They're just . . . well, you've seen how they are.'

'They seem normal to me,' I say.

'You don't have to lie.'

'Well, okay. They're probably from a perfectly nice planet.' It's out of my mouth before I realise it. I can't believe I said it.

Angelica looks at me strangely. That corner light in her eye glows a dull silver. I think she's going to get really angry. Then she throws her head back and laughs. 'I'd rather have that!' she says. 'I'd rather have someone joke about them than pretend everything with them is normal, then never speak to me again!'

I laugh along with her. Thing is, I wasn't joking when I said it. It just sort of slipped out. 'Is that what people do?'

She stops laughing. 'Often.'

'That's sad.'

'Well.' She sighs. Then she lies back on her bed. 'Doogie, if you want to kiss me again, they won't disturb us.'

She looks really pretty lying on the bed. I do want to kiss her, but I think if she is going to suck my brains out with her tongue or do whatever it is that aliens do to their victims, then this is the perfect opportunity for her. I mean, you know, come into my parlour said the spider to the fly. But then I guess that if she was going to do something like that she would have done it at the playground when we spent an hour snogging.

Though it does occur to me that maybe they don't suck your brains out all in one go. What if it's all a slow process? A bit at a time. What if by snogging they are leaving, like, small traces of some slow-acting poison or drug inside you?

Something that contaminates your brain. This would add up, because since that evening in the park I haven't been able to think very much about anything at all except snogging her again. That would be the perfect system, to get you to come back for more and more, with the change happening to you so slowly you don't even notice, until finally you have become one of them or perhaps you have mated with one of them to produce hybrid offspring who would go on to dominate the entire planet.

'Well?' she says.

'Well what?'

'Are you going to kiss me again?'

'Maybe.'

'Maybe? Playing it cool, aren't you?'

Actually that's what DatingTips.com tells you to do. Play it cool. I'm still making a study of DatingTips.com for Matt: I just haven't told him yet.

It says when you've got a girl back to your own place or to your car or whatever (okay I haven't got a place of my own or a car, but that's because DatingTips.com is really aimed at older guys who need to get a feel or whatever) then you should make out that you're not too bothered about any of it at all.

So you've turned down the lights, selected the right music, created the mood and you are ready to pounce on her. Relax! Don't! That's what she's expecting and she'll be on her guard. So find something to divert your attention. Study the sports results, as if that's the most important thing on your mind right now. Tell her to be comfortable while you check your email. Phone a friend to check on your stock options. Trust us, this will drive her nuts! With the tables turned, she's going to be ready to pounce on you!

It's all very well but this puts me in a difficult spot. I don't want her to be mad for it. I don't think I could handle it, to be honest, if she's going to come clawing at me like a jungle cat. But if I hold back now and try to talk about Arsenal or Manchester United, she's going to get all steamed up. I think I'm going to have to go ahead and give her a cuddle just to keep the lid on things.

'Shall I come and lie down next to you?' I ask.

'Mmmmm.'

'Shall I take my shoes off?'

'Huh? Yes.'

I sit on the bed and slowly unlace my trainers. DatingTips.com states clearly that only a peasant would keep his shoes on when lying down on a bed. It also warns that a man looks completely ridiculous in socks and these should go too. 'Shall I take my socks off?'

'Huh? Not unless you're planning to cut your toenails or something.'

Guys, please, a word about socks. Socks are the most unsexy item of clothing in your entire wardrobe. If you are taking off your clothes, make sure that your socks are not the very last thing to go. When a girl sees a guy in nothing but socks there's only one thing she can do: laugh so hard that the snot runs down her nose. Man, you've blown it!

It's just as well I'm not planning to get that far anyway, so I leave the socks on and climb on to the bed.

She snuggles up to me, lays her head on my chest and closes her eyes. If Van Helsing was right and they are sex mad, she doesn't seem to be in too much of a hurry. It's a relief. I mean, here we are in her bedroom, on her bed, with the perfect opportunity and all she really wants to do is to lie next to me, and I admit I don't mind at all. Angelica smells terrific. I can breathe in the scent of her skin and I can smell the shampoo in her hair and it seems to mix together perfectly. I like the place where her dark hair joins her neck, and I want to touch it because it's like the place where the sea meets the sand, it's not one thing and not the other. I lean forward and kiss her neck just there, and she gives off a tiny shiver.

'I like that.'

I do it again. She wiggles happily. I feel happy, too. You know what? I start to think that even if this whole alien idea is true, then I think I might not even care.

She turns to me sleepily and she puts her lips against mine and we start kissing, and it's just like in the playground on the roundabout; we stay like that for ages, and it seems like the whole world is turning slowly around us, while time stops just for us. We seem to lie in each other's arms for just a few moments and yet for all time, and in the outside world maybe an hour goes by; because the phone on Angelica's computer table rings.

It's her mum, paging her. Dinner is ready, she says. Come and get it.

● ● ● ●

Jennifer seems to have made an effort. She tells me that Angelica doesn't bring friends home often enough and Angelica flashes me a look designed to warn me not to say anything. Anyway, books have been shoved aside from the dining table area and piled up a few inches away from the dining chairs. The table has been draped with something that looks like a hippie poncho and a little tea-light candle burns in the centre of the table.

'Now as a special treat,' Jennifer says, beaming at me with huge eyes behind her glassless specs, 'I've rolled you some sushi myself.'

Angelica looks at me, pleading. 'You do like sushi, don't you?'

'Of course he likes sushi,' Jennifer says. 'Everyone likes sushi. It's a family favourite here, Doogie. We had it all the time when we lived in Japan.'

'Errr,' I say, 'what is it?'

Jennifer lets her hands fall to her sides, and sits well back in her chair – like I've just told her that I've never seen the sea or watched the sun go down. 'You've never tried sushi? Dominic, this is terrible, he's never tried sushi!'

Dominic – Dad – the big sleepy bear alpha male has just shuffled up to the table. 'Who? Who's never tried sushi?'

'The Doogie!'

'The Doogie?'

'Yes, the Doogie! Never tried it!'

'Never tried it?'

'No. Never!'

'Never ever?'

I wonder how long this banter is going to go on for, when Jennifer goes, 'Angelica, tell him he's in for a treat.'

'You tell him,' says Angelica.

'Okay: Doogie you're in for a treat. I rolled it myself. Angelica loves it.'

'Pretty much,' Angelica says. 'And Mum is good at rolling it.'

I don't know what this talk of rolling is. The only food I

know that gets rolled is pastry. Or maybe cheeses in some weird village in the Cotswolds where they roll cheese down a hill, though I don't know why.

Anyway, we all sit down and then Jennifer serves it up. And you know what it is? Fish.

Raw. Fish.

I smile meekly. When really I want to go, hey, do you think my name is Gollum?

14

· · · · · · ·

Well, dinner is a bit of a disaster unless you consider not eating anything as fine. Of course they all scoff this disgusting raw fish like it's perfectly sane. All kinds of stuff. Raw eels. Raw salmon. Raw squid. Munching it down and behaving like it was normal. I don't say anything to Angelica, and I try to tuck away a bit of rice or lettuce that goes with all this blubber, but it's the sort of thing that can put you off a girl big-time. I mean what's her breath going to reek like after chomping on that little lot? There's no two ways about it: her mouth is gonna give out like an Eskimo's leftover lunch.

Maybe Van Helsing is right after all. I look at her dad sucking it down like a whale eating krill and her mum shovelling it all away and I think: that ain't human. I remember why I'm here. To take a look, that's why. His warning comes back to me, not to get involved, not to get drawn in. That's what she's doing cosying up to me on the bed isn't it? Trying to get me drawn in.

My problem is I'm just too easy.

I decide to make conversation. 'What are you working on at the moment, Mr Vinterland?'

He stops eating and looks up like someone just shot an

arrow into the middle of his plate. Then he looks round him to see who did it.

Jennifer bails him out. 'Doogie just asked you about your work, Dominic.'

He turns to me, staring hard at me for a few seconds, wrinkling his nose. Then he turns back to his wife. 'Is it all right for me to talk about it?' he asks her.

Beaming, she nods. 'When someone asks you, you can.'

'That's great!' he says. He looks happy to talk about what I thought might be a big secret. He tells me in great detail what he's doing. He tells me it's computer software engineering, right at the cutting edge. It's in the future. It's not tomorrow's computers but the day after tomorrow's. I can't understand a single word of what he says, but I know it's cutting edge and all that cos Jennifer keeps butting in to tell me that it is.

After half an hour of this Angelica suddenly says, 'That's enough, Dad. Doogie is getting bored.'

Dominic sits back in his chair. 'Well, he asked me, and I haven't finished telling him.'

'It's true,' Jennifer puts in. 'Your dad hasn't got to the really interesting bit.'

'I've told you before, Dad. When someone's eyes look like they've gone gluey it means they're not listening any more.'

He looks at my eyes. 'You're right,' he says to Angelica. Then he turns back to me. 'How's school?'

'Fine,' I say. 'Still fine.'

'I'm showing an interest,' he tells Angelica.

'Good, but show a new interest.'

'How am I doing so far?' he asks me.

'Good,' I say.

'You see I'm rubbish at small talk. Can't get the hang of it.'

'No,' I say, 'it's pretty tricky.'

'Very tricky,' he says. 'Much harder than computers.'

'Do you think I could look at the computers in your study?' I ask.

Everyone around the table freezes.

I mean I'd probably have got the same reaction if I'd asked Jennifer to show me her arse. They look at me like I'm evil.

'All I'm saying is . . .' I try, 'that I like computers.'

'No one, but no one goes in Dad's study,' says Angelica. 'Not even Mum. He cleans it himself. He keeps it in strict order.'

I don't believe it. I mean what kind of a house would that be if there was a room that no one was allowed in except for one person? It's pretty clear to me that they've all got something to hide.

Jennifer is certainly not stupid. She seems to read my thoughts. For the first time in the evening she takes off her blue spectacles without glass and she squints at me. 'It might seem odd, Doogie, but Angelica's dad has to have everything in perfect order. The tiniest thing out of place can distract him and stop him working. Even if a pen is picked up and put down in another place, it disturbs him and throws him off balance. Even if a chair is moved three centimetres to the left or right. You see he has a condition –'

'Asperger's Syndrome?'

'Yes, that's right. That's why he works at home. He has to avoid the chaos of a normal working environment. It means less chance for things to get disturbed. That's why no one goes into his office.'

'I understand,' I say, sounding very mature. But I'm think-ing: *yeh, a likely story.*

I mean what a great ruse to direct everyone away from his research. Make out that he's got this mental condition. Like Van Helsing said to me: they can use that to hide everything.

Jennifer begins stacking the plates. No one seems to have noticed that I hardly ate anything, whereas my mum would still be talking about the fact seven hours after the event. Oh, that's another thing: there's no pudding. No Battenberg cakes or apple pie and ice-cream or tinned fruit; nothing. That's suspicious. If they were a real family they'd have a proper pudding. I think the only thing they can eat is raw fish, and they know perfectly well if they tried to serve raw prawns with custard the jig would be up. So they're stumped, and we all have to go without.

'I'll go back and do a little bit more,' Dominic says, getting up from his chair.

'Oh no!' goes Jennifer. 'Not when we have a guest. It's rude!'

'What happens next then?' he wants to know.

'Oh, God!' Angelica groans.

'Well there are a number of things,' Jennifer says. 'We can relax and discuss current affairs, art, history or any number of things. We can play a game.'

'Not that charades thing?' says Dominic.

'No, you're rubbish at that, darling.'

'The only way Dad can do it,' Angelica says by way of explanation, 'is to spell out the letters in the air.'

'But it's by far the quickest way if you're not allowed to speak!' he protests loudly.

'That's not the point, Dad!'

'So what is the point? I never do get the point of it.'

'One word, three letters, sounds like GUN,' says Angelica.

He looks blank. I can't help myself, so I say, 'Fun.' Even though I think charades is a stinking game and not fun at all.

'Fun? Oh, that. Fun.'

'Well, let's everyone sit down and I'll make us all a cup of tea. That's what people do now.'

It strikes me that every single thing the Vinterlands are trying to do is to make it look like they are a normal family. I suddenly have the feeling they wouldn't be doing any of this if I weren't there. They wouldn't eat together, sit together or even talk much together if I wasn't there. They are all hell-bent on passing themselves off as human beings, and only Angelica is making a decent job of it.

It also suddenly occurs to me that maybe *she* is the leader of the hive and not the big hulking father after all. That would be so clever. Make her look like the youngest and least threatening. It follows that she's the only one who goes out. Dominic and Jennifer stay at home all the time and don't mix. She's the one who lures people back, but for what purpose? Pretty soon I'm going to have to make my excuses and leave but I wonder if I might just get a tiny peek of his mysterious study before I do.

Jennifer goes out to make a brew, leaving the three of us to sit on the dusty old sofas in the lounge. There is an uncomfortable silence while we wait for the tea to arrive.

'Dominic looks hard at me. 'How's school?'

Angelica yawns. 'Dad, we've done all that.'

'Have we?'

'Several times.'

'Sorry.'

Angelica, Dominic and I sit in silence until the tea arrives. I'm looking forward to a cuppa to get the taste of blubber out of my mouth. But when Jennifer pours it and hands me a cup it doesn't look like any kind of tea I've seen before. In fact it looks like there's a load of hedge clippings in the bottom of the cup.

Jennifer gives me one of her goofy grins. 'Green tea,' she says proudly. 'From China.'

Right. Well China can keep it. I'd rather have proper tea from England.

Jennifer takes a slurp of her own tea. 'I know,' Jennifer says brightly. 'Let's play the alphabet game. What we do, Doogie, is go through the alphabet backwards and in turn think of the most unusual or funny word we can. I'll start. Ziggurat.'

'Yurt,' says Dominic.

'Xenophobe,' Angelica says softly. But she's watching me very intently throughout all of this. She obviously doesn't want to play this game but for some reason she doesn't object to it either.

'The Doogie's turn!' says Jennifer.

'Wigwam,' I say. It's pretty much all I can think of.

'Velutinous.'

'Upsilon,' shouts Dominic. 'How long do we have to play this for?'

'About half an hour I would think,' says Jennifer. 'That would be about right, wouldn't it, Angelica? You know these things – how long would a family do this for?'

'About half an hour,' she says in her quiet voice, still staring at me. 'But maybe not the same game.'

'Half an hour, Dad,' says Jennifer, 'and then you can go back to your computer.'

We continue to play this stunning game. We get to A and then we have to work back again to Z. Then we play another game involving numbers, where you have to shout out a funny word on multiples of three and five. It does my head in. I'm useless at it. It's an incredible relief when Jennifer calls the half-hour. I mean she looks at her wristwatch and calls the thing over at exactly the half-hour, not a minute over or under. Then she declares that Dominic can go back to his study and that Angelica and I can go back upstairs. Dominic is out of there in a flash. I tell you that big lumbering alpha male can move like a rocket when he wants to.

Jennifer goes out to stack the dishwasher, leaving Angelica and me in the lounge. 'You okay?' she says.

'Yeh, sure. Ha ha! Why wouldn't I be? Ha ha. No, I'm fine.'

'I know that was hard for you. But honestly that was even harder for them. They were making an effort for you. They don't know how to be around people. Really, they've no idea. They're happy with each other but they're hopeless in company.'

I have to think about what she is saying. Is Angelica coming close to confessing to me about what her parents really are? Isn't she as good as admitting to their extraterrestrial origins? She looks a bit sad. But I can't stand it any more. I have enough information to confirm what Van Helsing suspected and although I don't feel in any danger I want to go home. It's all too stressful. And that weird green Chinese tea is running right through me. I tell Angelica I need to pee and she tells me where the bathroom is.

As I pass along the hall I see Dominic come out of his study ahead of me and drag himself upstairs. I notice that he's left his study door ajar. I wait for a moment by the study door to see if he might come back at once. He doesn't. I nudge open his study door.

The room is awash with an eerie blue light. I push the door open a little further and I'm amazed at what's in the study. Three huge plasma screens dominate the room at centre, right and left of a workstation that is more like the comfortable flight-deck of a spacecraft compared to your normal crappy vinyl and chipboard computer-stand. The blue light is coming from the three screens and the rest of the room is low-lit by wall lamps.

But what really makes my jaw drop is what's running on the screens. It's like code, fast-running code of numbers and symbols. Strings of numbers and letters running like sand from the top of the screens to the bottom. But what's really strange is that as these figures tumble across the screen they form a recurring pattern. Over and over and very rapidly the figures form an outline image of an ape that begins to walk upright and then starts evolving into a caveman and then into a modern man and then into a —

'Hey! WHAT ARE YOU DOING IN HERE????'

It's Dominic, standing behind me, face like a thundercloud.

'Nothing! Honestly, the door was open and I was just coming to say goodbye.'

'NO ONE COMES IN HERE!' he roars at me. 'NO ONE.'

Next moment he's joined by Jennifer, and then Angelica. 'Oh no,' says Angelica, 'you didn't go in his room, did you?'

'I was just —'

'NO ONE!' he booms. His voice vibrates the walls.

'Why did you have to go and do that, Doogie?'

'I can't believe,' says Jennifer, her round eyes huge behind her glassless specs, 'that we invite you here as a guest, give you a hand-rolled sushi supper and . . . and . . . and the best Chinese tea and you repay us by snooping round the house. I can't believe that!'

'NO ONE!'

'I was just saying goodbye!' I blurt again.

'No, you weren't,' Angelica says. 'You were snooping.'

'No! I wasn't! Look, I have to go! It's time for me to go! My mum and dad are expecting me!' I manage to push my way past Dominic and get out into the hall.

Jennifer grabs my arm. 'You're not going before we get a full explanation of your behaviour!'

It's too late. They know that I've found them out. They realise I know what they all are, and it changes everything. The thought of what they might do to protect that information makes me panic. I wriggle free from Jennifer's weak grip and run down the hall, grabbing my coat as I go.

'Stop him!' Jennifer shouts.

Angelica comes after me, but I manage to get the front door open before she can do anything. I slam the door behind me and turn to run off into the night, but in my haste I crash my shin straight into a giant plant pot. I let out a shriek of pain and go spinning sideways. I trip. I put out a hand to break my fall but it's still tangled in my coat. I go down with a thud as my head strikes a kerbstone on the driveway, and everything fades to black.

● ● ●

When I come round I'm on a bed. Dominic, Jennifer and Angelica are standing over me. An orange light is pulsing behind them. They are staring at me. I pass out again.

• • • •

When I come round for the second time, the three of them are still standing over me. My head hurts. I realise there is some metal contraption strapped to my head. I move my hand up to touch my head but Angelica stops me. Dominic is holding something. It's like a massive syringe, but it's not like a syringe you get from the doctor's. It's a big fat glass-and-steel tube thing, about a foot long with a needle at one end. He leans over and inserts the needle into the side of my head, at my right temple. The orange light pulses behind them as I begin to slip out of consciousness again, but not before I see Angelica dig her thumbs into the skin folds under her chin and tug over her head the rubberised mask that I took to be her face. I don't get to see what's underneath the mask before I black out.

15

·······

When I come round for a third time, Mum and Dad are at my bedside. But this time I'm in a different bed. I'm in hospital. Dominic, Jennifer and Angelica are standing at the foot of the bed, watching nervously. I've got a thumping headache and the place where Dominic jabbed me with his glass-and-steel tube contraption is smarting really bad. I float a finger in their general direction though I find it hard to point accurately. 'Esha trreshtials,' is all I can manage and the act of speaking sends a whopping wave of pain through my head.

A doctor in a white coat appears. He's wearing a polka-dot dicky bow. 'Ah! You're awake, young man. Do you know where you are?'

'oshpital,' I manage to slur.

The doctor holds my face in his hands and rolls back my eyelids. He nods and lets me go. 'You've had a rather nasty crack to the head, young man. Gave us all a bit of a scare. You might have a bit of a headache but apart from that I don't think there's too much to worry about.' He turns to Mum. 'I'll run a few tests to check for concussion, then I think you'll be able to take him home.'

'Our Doogie!' Mum says, her face full of concern. 'What

have you been up to?'

'Oooh ya!' says Dad. 'Diving header, Doogie.'

'I'm glad he seems all right,' says Jennifer. 'I'm so sorry this happened.'

'Not your fault at all, Jennie,' says Mum. 'You've been marvellous and thank you for looking after him. Listen, there's no need for you to wait around any longer. Get yourselves off home, eh?'

'Only if you're sure.'

'Yes, he'll be fine now. And thanks again for everything.'

Angelica steps forward and gives my hand a squeeze before they leave.

I want to say to her: got your mask back on? But it comes out as, 'Gorra mash bashon?'

She lifts a hand in the air, shoulder high, and wiggles her fingers at me. Then I watch the three of them leave slowly, as if reluctant to go at all. My head throbs.

Later, while Mum and Dad go and get a cup of tea from a vending machine, the doctor performs some routine tests on me, asking me to count backwards, shining a light into my eyes, that sort of thing. At least the dizziness is fading and my normal speech seems to be returning. While Mum and Dad are away I take the opportunity to ask the doctor some questions. 'Can you do a blood test on me?'

'What for?'

I check round the ward to make sure no one is listening. 'Okay, this is going to sound weird. But someone pumped something into my blood while I was unconscious.'

'Don't worry. We don't do such things.'

'It's not you I'm talking about!'

'Who then?'

'Look, do you see anything odd about this cut on my head?'

He examines it again. 'Well, it is an unusual abrasion. But it's just where you fell and cracked your nut. It might leave a tiny scar but nothing to worry about for a handsome chap like you.'

'Can't you see a puncture mark? Maybe a round hole where something might have been injected?'

'What on earth are you talking about?'

'See those three people? The ones who came in with my mum and dad?'

He nods. 'You were at their house when you had your accident, right?'

'Yes. But they did something to me while I was out.'

His face suddenly becomes wreathed in smiles. 'Listen to me. You've had a nasty crack and your temperature went shooting up. You were concussed for a while and let me tell you that can give you some pretty hairy dreams. Believe me.'

'How do you know it was dreams?'

'I'm a doctor, young man. I'm paid to know.'

I give up. There's no point trying to tell him. He's convinced I was just dreaming it all. I might as well tell him the aliens have landed in Town Hall Square for all the good it will do me.

The doctor is staring at me now. Calculating. He's deciding what to do with me. It's then it occurs to me: what if he is one of *them*? I mean, I don't actually think he is, but what if he was? Anyway I dismiss the idea. I just want to go home.

'You'll be all right,' says the doc. Then he gets up and swings down the ward. I notice he has a funny walk. He's sort of bandy-legged. But I suppose that doesn't make him an alien.

• • • •

When I get home I get a bit of the old cotton-wool treatment. This means a couple of days off school and I can lie on the sofa while Mum runs round bringing me drinks and cakes and plumping up the pillows. The only bad thing about it is that I have to watch daytime TV, which is dreck. I'd really like to go to my room and fool around on the Internet, maybe get a message to Van Helsing, look at MongTube, things like that. But I'm supposed to be not well enough for that, so I have to watch telly. After a while I feel my brain start to soften. I wonder if it's something to do with what they injected into me, but I know it's more likely just the effects of daytime telly.

At the end of the second day Dad comes home from work covered in plaster dust. He stands over me, his nose wrinkling. 'Milking it a bit, aren't you?'

'What?' I say, in a tiny voice.

'I said you're milking it. Making Mum dance round you.'

'What?'

'Do you realise I was working for a living when I was your age?'

'What?'

'What what what?' he quacks. 'You're a bloody ponce, Doogie.'

Mum comes in from the kitchen to rescue me. 'What's up?'

'Him. He's a faker. He can go to school tomorrow.'

'Oh, he's only one day to go and it's the weekend. He might as well have the day off again.'

'He's a little shyster. A phony. A trickster.'

'Want a cup of tea?' Mum says brightly. 'What's put you in a bad mood, anyway?'

Dad points a plaster-dusted finger at me. 'I'm on to you, matey. Just remember that. I'm on to you.'

I know exactly what's put Dad in this mood. He's been thinking about the conversation he will have had with Angelica's mum and dad. They will have told him how my accident came about, though they will have put a bit of a spin on it to make it look like I was up to no good. And Dad will have been thinking about that. He's slow, like me. But like me he gets there eventually.

At tea that evening he brings up the subject. We're having steak-and-onion pie with oven chips and gravy. 'So then, Doogie, what were you doing snooping in whatsisface's office?'

'I wasn't snooping.'

'Yes, you bloody were.'

'Wasn't.'

'Anyone want a bit more pie?' says Mum.

'You don't go poking round people's private work places,' Dad says. He has a fibre of steak caught between his teeth. 'You just don't.'

'I was looking for Mr –'

'Not very nice, our Doogie,' Mum says, 'after people have invited you into their homes.' Mum says this very gently. It's not often she sides with Dad when he's having a go at me. 'Not very nice.'

'I was just going to say goodbye!' I feel the blood rush to my face. My cheeks are flaming. I can hear my voice go sort of squeaky. 'You always tell me to be polite! Not very polite if you just sod off home without saying goodbye, is it? Not very good manners! Not very nice –'

'Stop talking rubbish,' says Dad. 'You'll call them up on the phone and you'll apologise for creeping round.'

'But –'

'No buts. You'll phone and apologise. That's it.'

'Mum!'

'Your dad's spoken,' says Mum, in a way that means they've discussed this between themselves before they sat down to dinner.

I think: *what's that?* Dad's spoken? Is he like Moses or something? But I look at the bit of steak between his chomping teeth and I decide not to say anything.

'Now. Anyone want more pie?' Mum asks.

16

Dad hath spoken; and with Dad standing over me I have to call the Vinterlands and apologise to all three of them in turn. It's a ridiculous conversation. Ridiculous. First I speak to Angelica, who hears me out pretty much in silence. Then Jennie, who keeps going, 'Hmmmmmm,' as if she doubts whether I really mean it. Then finally to the scary alpha male, who listens – I guess – in complete silence. I have to keep saying, 'Are you still there, Mr Vinterland?' to which he responds with a grunt. Then at a certain point he just hands the phone back to Jennie. I mean that is rude. Ignorant. It doesn't matter whether someone was snooping round your study or not. If they're trying to apologise and you just grunt and hand back the phone to someone else, well, that's the last time I'll let them drag me round to their place for tea.

With Jennie going hmmmmmm all the time there seems to be no end to this conversation. I mean I blab on for hours about how I'm sorry but there's no cut-off. She doesn't say oh let's forget it or let's draw a line under that and start again or those kind of things any normal human being would say. She just lets it drift. Hmmmmm. For God's sake. But that's my point: they're not normal human beings.

Anyway to get out of all that I ask if I can speak to

Angelica again. I hear her say, 'Do you want to speak to him?' and I hear Angelica say, 'No.' 'Oh go on,' says Jennie. 'All right,' says Angelica. Then Angelica comes on the line and says, 'Bye, Doogie.' And she hangs up on me!

Now that is just pig-in-the-trough-ignorant!

Dad has more or less lost interest by now. He has stepped over to the window and is staring out of it, arms folded, with only half an ear to my end of the conversation. He doesn't know they've hung up on me, so I keep talking into the mouthpiece. 'Well, I'm relieved you accept my explanation of why I was in Mr Vinterland's office. Yes, it did look a bit like I was poking around, but I'm happy now that you see that I wasn't doing what you thought I was doing but in actual fact I wasn't. Yes, yes, yes, of course, I will tell my father that you are satisfied with what I've told you.'

Dad suddenly spins round and looks at me suspiciously.

'Thank you and goodbye,' I say quickly, and then just before I put the phone down for some reason I say, 'God speed to you too, Mrs Vinterland,' before clattering the phone back in its cradle.

Dad twitches his nostrils at me. God speed. That was a line too far, I think.

'Well, that's done,' I say.

'You know what you need?' Dad says. 'You need a little job for your spare time. Keep you out of mischief.'

• • • •

Van Helsing: We need you to hang in there, Holmwood. You're doing sensational work. You've got more information from one visit to their hive than we've uncovered in the last two years. Bravo to you!

Me: Well, she won't even speak with me now.

Van Helsing: Make up with her. Go back there tomorrow.

Me: I can't.

Van Helsing: Why not? It's Saturday. You don't have school.

Me: My dad found me a Saturday job.

Van Helsing: Doing what?

Me: Shovelling sand and gravel at a builders' yard owned by his mate. I have to go there at nine o'clock tomorrow morning and work all day.

Van Helsing: I can't believe that someone with your talents is going to be shovelling sand and gravel.

Me: That's what I said. My dad just laughed at me. I'll be getting £4.50 an hour.

Van Helsing: That much, eh? Well at least we all appreciate you here, Holmwood. I mean that.

Me: Look, can't we meet to talk about the things that happened to me?

Van Helsing: I've told you we can't meet. It's absolutely out of the question. They'll be tracking you now, keeping a record of everyone you make contact with.

Me: How do you know that?

Van Helsing: When you woke up and witnessed them injecting you, they weren't taking blood samples from you at all.

Me: No?

Van Helsing: No. They were inserting a chip.

Me: ????????????????

Van Helsing: A microchip. You're not the first. We have a couple we've successfully removed. It's tiny. No more than a few filaments. Under a microscope you can see what looks like a bar-code on the filaments. That small scar in the side of your head is where they inserted it.

Me: Christ!!!

Van Helsing: Don't panic, Holmwood.

Me: Don't panic? I'm gonna get it out, right now!

Van Helsing: *Don't touch it!*

Me: Why not? I can get my mum to get it out with tweezers.

Van Helsing: Repeat DO NOT TOUCH IT! Do not attempt to get it out yourself. It's a delicate procedure. We can do it. As I say, we've done it a couple of times already. There's no hurry.

Me: WHAT DO YOU MEAN NO HURRY? It's all right for you!

Van Helsing: Don't panic! They can't activate it for at least twelve weeks.

Me: Activate it? What? Why not?

Van Helsing: It's organic. They have to wait until it has grafted with the living tissue of your brain.

Me: What the —

Van Helsing: Holmwood, you're safe. What they inserted into your brain was not a bit of machinery. It's more sophisticated than that. The chip is a living thing but it's just incubating in your brain right now.

Me: Incubating? INCUBATING?

Van Helsing: Yes. When your brain tissue has absorbed it completely, it will reach out fibrous tendrils to connect with the neurons in your brain.

Me: SOD OFF! SOD OFF! SOD OFF!

Van Helsing: You're upset.

Me: Yeh, you could say that!

Van Helsing: Don't be.

Me: It's all right for you! You're the one who told me to go

various building supplies like bricks, breezeblocks, paving slabs, bags of cement and larchlap fences scraped together in little pockets around a muddy drive. Chalky White, the proprietor, has an 'office' in a wooden potting shed. Dad takes me into the shed. Chalky is sitting at a filthy desk, drinking tea. There's a phone, a two-bar electric fire on the desk itself and a load of grubby invoices on a spike.

'Mornin', Chalky!' goes my dad, loud enough to be heard across the yard.

'His worshipfulness the mayor!' shouts Chalky, for reasons I don't understand. 'Rest your bones. 'Ave a cuppa. I just brewed it.' Chalky is a red-faced man with a close-cropped white beard. His white hair is close-cropped, too. His face looks like someone spent the last few weeks rubbing it down with sandpaper. He has dull blue eyes with heavy, sleepy eyelids. His fingertips are stained mustard and mahogany. He has the stub of a cigarette on the go at the moment, and he uses it to light another.

'Can't, Chalky. Got a race on. Just stuck my head in to bring you the lad.'

The lad. Me. Right.

'Oh, this is the little f'ker is it? Will I get any f'kin work out o' the little f'ker?'

'Stay on his case, Chalky, stay on his case.'

Chalky blows smoke in my direction and blinks at me. 'Can the little f'ker make tea?'

'He can't even wash his face, Chalky.'

'Oh! One of them f'ker's is 'e? We'll see about that then.'

For some reason, for some bloody reason, I'm smiling at all of this, like it's a big joke which I'm enjoying, which I'm not. But there I am, smiling like a prize prat, my cheeks aching from the effort I'm putting into smiling.

Dad turns to me. 'Put your back into it and don't let me down, okay, son?'

'Okay.'

He turns to Chalky. 'I'll leave him to your tender care, mush.'

'My tender care,' laughs Chalky. 'That's a good one. My tender care.'

When Dad has gone, Chalky sits drinking from his huge mug of tea, taking drags on his cigarette, blinking at me. I shuffle nervously. He takes another sip and blinks at me again. There's an old typist's chair in the shed and after a minute I go to sit down on it.

'No point f'kin sittin',' says Chalky, setting down his mug, 'you've come here to f'kin work.'

'I know,' I say. 'I mean, of course I have.'

'Well what you f'kin sitting down for?'

'I'm not.'

'Too right you're f'kin not. Follow me.'

Chalky marches me out of the potting shed and down the driveway to where a lorry is parked alongside a sand hopper. 'Stand f'kin back,' he says. He grabs a lever on the sand hopper and dumps a load of sand on the ground. 'Do you know what a f'kin yard of f'kin sand is?'

'Yeh. Course I do.'

'What is it then?'

'It's a yard by a yard by a yard of sand. I should know: my dad's a builder.'

Chalky nods, like fair enough. There is a shovel lying by the pile of sand. 'Chuck a f'kin yard o' f'kin sand on the back o' this f'kin lorry. And don't take all f'kin day.'

I get the shovel. It's huge. I mean if you filled the shovel full you'd never be able to lift it high enough to throw the sand on to the back of the lorry. I know what's going to happen. I'm going to get half a scoop on my shovel and Chalky is going to go f'kin f'kin f'kin. Luckily he's distracted when a beat-up old car draws up at the entrance to the yard.

'It's f'kin Nobby,' says Chalky. At first I think he says Noddy, but then I remember Dad saying that another old pal of his, Nobby, also works at the yard with Chalky.

Nobby is a huge gorilla of a man with tattoos – proper tattoos, of sailing ships and skulls and daggers – and his hair tied back in a pony tail.

'Mornin', Chalky-One-Kenobe!' shouts Nobby, booming across the yard like Dad. This must be what builders do, yell at each other all day long.

'His worshipfulness the mayor!' shouts Chalky. Then he says to me, 'I'll be back in a short while. You get that yard loaded.' Then he strides back down the driveway to join Nobby, and they both disappear inside the potting shed, probably for more tea, more cigarettes and more yelling.

I want to send a text message to Angelica. Firstly I want to ask her if she really has put an insect in my head. Because if she has, then that means that she never really had any true feelings for me at all, and the whole thing was faked from day one. And I just don't believe that. You don't go spinning in slow circles on a roundabout with someone you don't care about. You just don't.

I really do need to talk with her. For one thing, if she has done something to my head – and I'm pretty certain that she has – then she's probably the only person who can help me. She would know how to reverse it. Or whatever. I need to find out if she really does have feelings for me, in which case she wouldn't want me to come to any harm. I can't believe she would have just tricked me. I can't believe that. Whatever happens, I need to persuade her that we should get back together.

I remember something I read on DatingTips.com. It said you should always appear busy, like you've got a million other things to think about besides her, so that your girlfriend will think you're meeting hundreds of other hot chicks. So I think it will sound pretty cool if I tell her I'm at work. That I have a Saturday job. Well obviously I'm not going to tell her that it's a job shovelling sand at a builders' yard that looks like a nuclear accident has devastated the area; obviously not. She's not going to fall for the idea that dozens of hot babes are out here with me shovelling sand and gravel, is she? So I'll just tell her the minimal. That's what DatingTips.com says: tell women the minimal.

I take my phone out and start to compose a text. Then I think maybe I should get a bit of sand on the back of the lorry first, just in case cheerful Chalky forgets to smoke another cigarette or yell at Nobby and comes out to check up on me instead. So I put my phone away and pick up the shovel.

Like I say the shovel is huge. A lot heavier than a mobile phone, too. Plus the sand is a bit wet from the rain, and the back of the lorry seems to be unusually high. After a few shovels, my arms start to ache. But I'm not going to wimp out. I've got a point to prove to the old man. I decide to keep loading until the job is done, and after that I'll send my text to Angelica. After about half an hour I've loaded a yard of sand on to the back of the lorry. My muscles are screaming but at least I've done it. I throw on another half a shovel just for good measure, throw the shovel back into the pile of sand, and pull the phone out of my pocket.

I'm just about to text the message when Chalky and Nobby spill out of the potting shed. They start walking the other way then Chalky seems to remember me and they both start walking towards me, so I pocket my phone and pick up the shovel again to look busy.

'Nobby, this is Doogie,' Chalky shouts. 'His worshipful mayor.'

'All right, son,' shouts Nobby, with a scouser accent. 'You fit?'

They draw abreast of the lorry. Chalky sniffs at the sand I've loaded on the back. 'What's this?' he says.

'Yard of sand.'

''Kin hell,' says Nobby.

'That's f'kin not a f'kin yard o' f'kin sand!' says Chalky. 'Gimme the f'kin shovel, you useless f'ker.'

This is pretty much how it goes all morning. Everything they ask me to do is watched, mocked and generally treated as hilarious entertainment. They particularly enjoy seeing me try to load three-foot-by-two-foot paving slabs on to the back of the lorry. It has them doubled up.

'This is better than the telly!' Nobby keeps yelling, slapping the thigh of his torn jeans. 'Better than the telly.'

'What f'kin planet is he f'kin from!'

It gets on my nerves but they're not nasty with it. In fact they stop every now and again to offer me cigarettes, which I refuse; and to tell me crude jokes which I don't always get but which I pretend are real funny. Seems like the worst crime you can commit at Chalky's Building Supplies is not to laugh at someone else's joke. I try telling a joke but I screw it up. They laugh along anyway.

Mid-morning I have to go out on the lorry with Nobby to drop off a load of sand, concrete and slabs. The lorry cab is littered with foil pie trays, empty cigarette packs, old newspapers and a couple of porn magazines. There are also three or four paperback books, all science fiction with spaced-out cover artwork. I pick one up.

'You like sci-fi?' Nobby says, changing gears at a junction.

'Dunno.'

'Love it, I do. Always got one on the go, I have. Great when you're waiting around. Love it.'

'Are they about aliens?'

'Not all of them. Some.'

'I'm interested in the idea of aliens,' I tell him.

He looks at me. I wish he'd keep his eyes on the road while he's driving. The lorry clatters along. 'Really?'

'Yes.'

'Why?'

'Dunno.'

'Well,' says Nobby, 'you're looking at someone who has experienced one in real life.'

'What?' I say.

Now he suddenly keeps his eyes fixed on the road. His voice drops. 'Yeh. I actually had what is called a close encounter of the first kind.'

'Really? I'd like to hear about it.'

'Nah. I don't like talking about it.'

I'm on the verge of telling him about my own experiences. But something tells me it's the wrong moment. 'Go on,' I say, 'I'm interested.'

Nobby stares at the road ahead. His mood has changed.

He reaches across the cab and grabs a tatty porn magazine which he throws into my lap. 'Nah. Change the subject.'

At lunchtime I have a thermos flask and the ham sandwiches packed by Mum. Chalky and Nobby brew up even more tea and the three of us sit in the potting shed.

'What you got?' says Chalky.

'Ham.'

'What you got, Nobby?'

'Cheese.'

'Anyone want to trade for a fish paste?'

'F'k off,' says Nobby.

I say nothing. We chew in silence until Chalky says, 'How was he, Nobby?'

'He's a good lad.'

Chalky looks at me with his dead-fish blue eyes. 'Watch out for Nobby, son. He'll start telling you all about his adventures with little green men.'

My ears prick up. 'He wouldn't tell me the story.'

Nobby's eyes roll.

'Tell 'im,' says Chalky.

'Get stuffed,' Nobby says. 'You never take it seriously anyway.'

'F'kin tell 'im!'

'Nah.'

'Nobby had a run in the woods, didn't you, Nob? Coming back from the pub after twelve pints of wallop.'

'It wasn't after twelve pints. I'd had a few but I wasn't drunk.'

'What happened?' I ask.

'I don't like talking about it.'

'Tell 'im!' barks Chalky.

Nobby sighs. He puts his mug of tea down and wags a finger at me. 'You take the mickey and I'll slap your ear for you.'

'I won't.'

'I might,' says Chalky.

'But I won't,' I say again.

Nobby sniffs. He pulls a string of dried snot from his nose and inspects it before flinging it aside. 'I'd been up the Red Lion and I never drive after drink cos you risk losing your licence. So I walk across the field and take a short cut through the woods. Well, we'd had a lock-in at the Red Lion and it was about one o'clock in the morning, and I was crashing through the woods and there was this bright light.'

I glance up at Chalky who, even though he's heard this story before, is listening intently. He nods at me.

'Brilliant white light,' Nobby continues, 'cutting through the trees. So I think what the hell is this.' Nobby pauses to light a cigarette. He offers me one and I refuse for about the tenth time that morning. He takes a deep drag, puts back his head and blows out a long draught of smoke. 'Well I go over to have a look. There's smoke and light, and it's so bright I can't make it out. Then the light starts flickering and the next thing is I come round and I'm lying on a table.'

I sit up at that. Nobby notices my reaction and he turns to me. I want to shout that I know where this story is going, because I've been there! But I don't say anything. Nobby's voice has got lower and lower and I'm leaning towards him, listening hard.

'Anyway next to the table is this grey figure standing over me. I'm a bit groggy, only half awake, but this grey figure is sticking its long bony finger in my ear and wiggling it about. I can hardly move. I ask him to stop but he doesn't. Then I get angry and I say if you don't stop doing that I'll get off this table and kick you in the genitals. And this grey figure looks at me and says: we don't have genitals where we come from. I say what? No genitals? So how do you have sex? And the grey figure goes: like this . . .' And here Nobby sucks his finger, leans over and jams his thick wet finger in my ear.

'Ow!' I shout.

Nobby and Chalky are shrieking with laughter now. They're red in the face and howling.

'Very funny,' I say. 'Very funny.'

This only makes them laugh more. Chalky slithers off his chair and on to his knees, holding his ribs. Nobby is laughing so hard he has snot running down his nose. 'Hooo-hooo-hooo! Like this! Hoo-hooo-hoo!'

'Yeh, very funny.'

It takes them about three hours to stop laughing at me. They wipe their eyes, look at each other and then start again.

'You're like a pair of schoolkids,' I say. But for some reason this just starts them off again, so I sit there with my arms folded.

'Here,' says Nobby. 'Have a f'kin ciggie.'

'No thanks.'

● ● ● ●

In the afternoon I shovel more sand and gravel and load more slabs. I do another two deliveries. Every time Chalky walks by – with or without a customer at his side – he looks at me, sticks his finger in his mouth and then points it at me before walking away, chuckling.

Dad comes to pick me up at five o'clock.

'His worshipfulness the mayor!' shouts Chalky.

'How's he been, Chalk-o?'

'He's a good lad. Bit slow on the shovel. But he can take a joke. Here, son.' Chalky reaches into his pocket and pulls out a huge roll of ready cash. He counts out my wages. It's over thirty quid. It's my first wages, ever. It feels good. It feels really good.

'That feel good?' says Dad.

'No,' I say.

'Same time next week?' Chalky says to me.

'Right,' I say.

Dad winks at Chalky.

As we're driving home Dad says, 'Well, your first day's work. How was it?'

'Can I ask you a question, Dad?'

'Sure you can.'

'Is f'kin work f'kin always like f'kin that?'

He takes his eyes off the road for a second to look at me. Then he refocuses on his driving. 'Don't tell yer mum, though, eh?'

17

• • • • • • •

I'm left facing a Saturday evening with a pocket full of money and no one to spend it on. I haven't had time to text Angelica and I don't know what kind of a response I would get. I desperately need to get in touch with her and spend some time with her. Firstly because I would like to plead with her to get this thing out of my head. Secondly because – I admit it – I'm missing being with her.

Oddly the two things seem connected and I wonder if there is something in the chip that is sending out some sort of signal to make me want her more than I would have done. I could ask Van Helsing about that but I'm pretty disgusted with him at the moment.

I check out DatingTips.com to see what advice it has for getting back in the girl's good books. Like I said, it has a section called What To Do If She Dumps You.

Women dump guys for two reasons only. One) she's testing you, or two) she really wants to dump you. If it's (one) there are a couple of things you can do. If it's (two) Nothing in the world can help you get back someone who doesn't want to be with you: except perhaps money. Does that make women sound shallow? Deal with it! If you don't have any money you can always pretend, but since it will only take her a few days to find out, you might as well not bother. Move on, dude!

I don't know if this can be true. How would it work? She dumps you and you wave a wad of notes in front of her face and she starts patting her hair and going *oooooh ooooh I was only joking*. I can't see that. What guy would fall for that? And what guy would even want someone like that to come back to him?

Sometimes I'm not sure about this DatingTips.com. Anyway I'm only really checking it out for Matt.

So unless she's just testing you, you may as well GIVE UP, my friend. But if she's just testing you, stay cool. NEVER beg. Make out you have a hundred hot babes you could spend your time and money on. Only then should you remember that she likes the theatre and casually mention that you have two tickets for a show that are going to waste. Tell her you'd bought them before she dumped you, as a surprise. Tell her that she can have both tickets to take her new boyfriend along to a show. Say you don't mind at all, not a bit. And then when she says that she hasn't got a new boyfriend (she's lying, dude, but let's gloss over that for the moment) that's when you casually say oh well the two of us should just go along as 'friends'. If she says yes to this it's all back on again. Because in women's coded language going out together as friends is NOWHERE. She would never have said yes, so that has to leave you SOMEWHERE.

I dunno, it all sounds a bit complicated, and really not much use since Angelica has never once said anything to me about liking the theatre. And why would I have two tickets? The only time I've ever been to the theatre was on a school trip and it was pants.

The other thing that DatingTips.com recommends, on the basis that you are being tested rather than dumped, is to spend a lot of time and attention on another girl. And if you flash the cash at this other girl, well, that gets the first girl spitting mad, and according to DatingTips.com she's back at your side like a greased whippet.

I spend the evening thinking about it while watching TV with Mum and Dad. I have to fend off Mum's daft questions. You could set your watch by my mum. Every six minutes she thinks up a new one to interrupt our viewing.

'So did you enjoy your day in the builders' yard, our Doogie?'

'It was all right.'

Six minutes later. 'So will you go back next week?'

'Probably.'

Six minutes later. 'And you met Chalky, then?'

'Yes.'

Six minutes later. 'Good old Chalky.'

'Yes, good old Chalky.'

Six minutes later. 'Did you have lunch together?'

'Yuh.'

Six minutes later. 'And was your lunch all right?'

'Duh.'

What is it with mothers? I think they're the ones who have a chip in their brain. Probably at birth. I mean when they give birth. Probably the midwife slips the chip in when they're not looking so that they become a robot. I mean, why else would they clean up your sick and your poo and all that, and then make your sandwiches every day? I wouldn't if I was a mum. If I had a baby I'd tell it to clean up its own vomit, and make its own sandwiches.

Before going to bed I compose a couple of text messages for Angelica:

Hey, got cash, lets hang out!

But I don't send it. Then:

Oi! Get this f'kin thing outa my head or else!

But I don't send that either.

• • • •

Back at school on Monday I see Matt dancing around Shelly Hobbs. Yeh, she of the big bazongas. He's making a tool of himself again. Flicking his hair back and tripping over his own heels trying to be funny. I tell you it pains me to see a good mate in such a state.

Anyway, as I'm watching Matt flapping around Shelly Hobbs I get an idea. I mean she's the obvious person to apply the DatingTips.com programme to. For getting Angelica back, I mean. Because Angelica is bound to think that I'm mad for Shelly's bazongas, and what with Angelica only having small bazongas it should work.

As it happens on Monday morning before the school bell Angelica is leaning her back against the bike-shed wall. She has an iPod in her ear. A few yards away, also leaning against the bike-shed wall is Shelly Hobbs, still being 'entertained' by Matt and Tonga. Well, mostly Matt making a goat of himself trying to get Shelly to laugh while Tonga hangs in there baring his teeth at them in what is supposed to look like a grin.

I walk straight up to Shelly and wave my cash under her nose. 'I've been working my socks off all weekend just so that I can take you out.'

Yeh, it's pretty brazen. But it's a line I took from Dat-ingTips.com

> **Never ask a girl for a date outright. Instead, make a statement that will get a reaction. That way she can't actually say no. Because if she comes back with some put-down line like, *well you've wasted your time*, then you can snap back with, *but I decided to raise my standards and ask someone else.***

Well it does get a reaction. Shelly goes red. Not just red, but fire-engine red. Her eyelashes flutter weirdly.

Matt stops his dancing and clowning around. He just stares at me, chewing his lip, and so does Tonga. They look at me like a pair of cornered rats. Angelica is pretending to fiddle with her iPod but I know she's watching me like a hawk. Or maybe like an android with a high-tech optical burner where an eye should be.

'Where you been working?' Shelly asks me, recovering.

'Builders' yard. Shovelling sand and gravel. Loading slabs.'

'Intit 'ard work?'

'Yep. But you just keep your mind on all the money at the end of it.' I hear myself repeating what my dad says about it.

Shelly gets her confidence back. 'You must have big muscles then.'

'Maybe.'

She steps over to me. 'Can I feel your muscles?'

'If you want.'

She gives my biceps a squeeze. 'Ooooh! What about the other one?' She gives my left biceps a squeeze. 'Hard muscles! Must be from lifting all that money.'

I can't think of an answer. I rack my brain to remember what DatingTips.com says you should say next. Then I remember it tells you to take the mickey. Apparently girls love it if you do that. 'Are you clever enough to know what time it is when the big hand is on the twelve and the little hand is on the four?'

'Four o'clock,' says Shelly.

'Smart girl. That's what time I'll be in Café Vienna.'

The morning bell goes and I'm away. I know that Shelly, Angelica, Matt and Tonga are all staring after me.

• • • •

At break time, trouble. Matt and Tonga corner me. They've dragged in Wilko, who keeps rubbing his eye like it's sore but really it's cos he's a bit embarrassed.

'What's goin' on?' Matt says.

'How do you mean?'

'We're supposed to be mates. All of us.'

'How do you mean?' I say again, all innocent.

'Mates', says Tonga, 'never make a move on each other's girls.'

'No,' Wilko adds. 'You shouldn't do that, Doogie.'

'Who you talking about?'

'You know who I'm talking about,' Matt says.

'Say it then,' I challenge him.

'You know perfectly well.'

'So are you talking about Shelly? So are you going out with Shelly?'

'Not exactly going out,' Matt says, 'but –'

'But what? If you're not going out you're not going out.' See, I know this. I know that they've never actually been out together, and I know he's never asked. I know this for a fact. Matt has spent weeks dancing around her, pulling silly faces, goofing around and trying to make her laugh and he's never once asked her out.

'You know perfectly well Matt has got his eye on Shelly,' Tonga says. 'You know that. So you don't make a move on your mate's –'

'Mate's what? What is she, exactly? What do you know about girls anyway, Tonga? The only girl you'd be interested in is one who would feed you a steady stream of meat pies and cream cakes. So butt out! And as for you, Matt, I'm not even interested in Shelly Hobbs.'

'Oh yeh? So why did you ask her out on a date?'

'I didn't ask her out on a date. If you kept your ears open instead of making a tit of yourself you'd have heard me say I would be in Café Vienna at four o'clock. Go and read DatingTips.com.'

'What?' says Matt, twisting up his face.

'What's that when it's at home?' says Wilko.

'You heard,' I say. 'Get up to speed, will ya?'

'You know what, Doogie?' Matt says with a sneer. 'I used to like you.'

● ● ● ●

For the next part of my plan I'm going to have to bite the bullet and earn a detention. I don't know how just yet and I'm still thinking about it at lunchtime when Angelica decides it's her turn to have a go. I'm walking down the corridor outside the IT rooms and she just blocks my way. 'That was cheap,' she says.

'What?'

'Cheap and tacky.'

'What was?'

'Cheap, tacky and most of all transparent.'

'What are you on about?'

'And all this *What? What?* stuff just makes you look pathetic. How long are you going to go through life pretending you haven't got a clue what people are talking about?'

'What?'

'Doogie, the reason I liked you so much is I thought you were a kind person and that you only pretended to be gormless. But now I'm wondering if you really are gormless. And unkind, too. And if you say what again, I swear I'll slap you.'

There's a light in her eyes that makes me think she means it. My mouth is trying to say *what* but I'm fighting it down.

She's not done. 'You've spent so long pretending to be thick that you now think everyone else is as thick as you pretend to be.'

'Eh?' I can't help it. It just comes out.

'You're not even interested in Shelly Hobbs. Why tease her like that? I hope it wasn't a sad attempt to make me jealous, because if it was it's just despicable.'

'Shelly Hobbs is all right.'

'Yes, she's all right, but you don't even fancy her. I know you don't.'

'What do you care? You've made it plain how you feel.'

'What do you expect, Doogie! You come to my house, and go snooping round in my dad's study when I've told you the terrible effect it has on him. Okay, he's weird but you were warned about that. It's completely thrown him off his work.'

'Never mind your dad,' I say, jerking a thumb at my small head wound. 'What about this?'

'That was your own doing.'

'My own doing? Get real, will you!'

'You brought that on yourself.'

'Are you going to help me get it out?'

This doesn't sound right when I say it, and what's worse is that Shelly Hobbs happens to walk past at that exact moment. 'Get you!' Shelly bellows. 'See you at Café Vienna, Mister Muscles.'

Angelica ignores her. 'What?'

'See, you say *what* too.'

'What did you say?'

'Going to deny it?'

'Deny what?'

'Exactly!'

I can't bring myself to say it again. The thing is, I have a moment of doubt. I look at Angelica and she looks like all her confidence has drained away. She looks angry and hurt and confused and . . . well . . . human. And even though I know that she and her people have inserted a chip into my brain it hits me that what I want most of all is just to hold her hand, to walk out of school, to go somewhere we can go to be alone together.

But that doesn't happen. Angelica suddenly turns on her heel and walks away from me, hitching her rucksack on her shoulder. I have to fight an instinct to run after her.

In class after lunch Angelica sits well away from me. Meanwhile Shelly spends the afternoon smirking and making eyes at me while Matt, Tonga and Wilko just scowl in my direction. Near the end of the first lesson I see Angelica take out her diary and write something in it.

I wouldn't mind getting a look at that diary. Though when I think about it I get a little squeeze of a headache from the area where the chip was put into my brain. I wonder if they have some system where they can read my thoughts, but then I remember Van Helsing telling me that the chip doesn't activate for several weeks. However, the headache does give me an idea and I get my chance at looking at Angelica's diary towards the end of the day.

The last period of the day is PE. Now normally I'm up for PE any time, happy to play soccer or shimmy up a rope in the gym or whatever is on the timetable, and our PE teacher Jones The Slap knows this. Jones The Slap, a bald-headed barrel-chested muscle-bound hulk is always threatening to give someone a slap, but never needs to. You wouldn't want to risk it, either.

He's a booming Welshman. 'Right, lads, anyone not changed in two minutes gets a slap. Why the long face, Doogie?'

He sees me holding a hank of hair to display the cut at my temple. 'I had to go to hospital for this and I've been getting migraines. I think I've got one coming on now.'

Jones looks at me doubtfully, hands on hips. Like I say, he knows I never bunk off PE. 'Okay, it's off to the library for you. As for the rest of you, anyone dragging their heels will be rewarded with a sharp slap!'

Thing is, the girls' gym is adjacent to the boys' gym, and on my way to the library I have to pass the row of pegs where they all hang their book-bags. And there, dangling from a peg, is Angelica's sky-blue bag.

A little look. Just a little look. Not to see if she's saying anything about me, but to see if there's any information that might help me get this thing out of my head. Any tips. Well, yes, to see if she's saying anything about me, too. Maybe. To indicate how she feels about me. That as well. A bit. I mean that's only fair since she won't actually come out up front and say what her feelings are. In which case anybody can be excused for looking inside another person's diary. That's only natural.

The row of coat-pegs is just outside the girls' gym so I can keep an eye on the door and see if anyone is coming. It's easy for me to duck behind the row of hanging rucksacks and backpacks and gym bags. I lift off Angelica's bag and unzip the pack. Her diary practically falls into my hand. It's as if she left it there deliberately. It's almost as if she wants me to read it.

I flick to the most recent entry, the one she wrote earlier today. In her incredibly neat handwriting it says:

> Tried to reason with Doogie today but as usual he played stupid and pretended not to understand anything. Then he just started talking rubbish. He has this chip and it gets the better of him.

● ● ● ●

There it is in black and white! A clear reference to the microchip they inserted into my brain! My hands start trembling. I flick back to see if she made a diary entry on the night I went round to her house. There isn't anything about what they did to me but I do find the following, all again in her perfect, neat handwriting.

> * Humans are social by nature and find meaning in relationships.
> * Human happiness is enhanced by friendship, which is the result of reciprocal goodwill.
> * Humans are an integral part of nature, the result of unguided evolutionary change.

* Humans' knowledge of the world is derived by observation, experimentation, and analysis.
* Humans are sometimes prepared to change their opinions in the light of new information presented to them. It is vital for Humans to have opinions, and to be prepared to change them, if necessary.

I don't really understand it. I mean, I don't know what it's saying about us exactly, but I know what it means. It means that Angelica and her hive are making a study of us. Who knows for what purpose? I try to read it a second time to get a clearer picture, but I don't get the chance.

'What the hell do you think you're doing?'

It's Annabelle Lugs, the girls' PE teacher. She's a wiry little fitness fanatic with close-cropped hair and ears that stick out really badly. I mean most people's ears live stream-lined to their skull but hers stick out at ninety degrees. You'd think she'd grow her hair to cover them up but she seems to want to make a feature of them. We didn't have to nickname her lugs — honestly, that's her name. Incredible really. She walks around with clenched fists, permanently angry, and she hates boys. Right now I'm getting the full force of that.

'Answer me!' she yells.

'Reading,' I say.

'I can see that, you oaf! Whose bag is that you're rooting through?' She flicks the name tag on the bag. 'Wait here!'

She marches to the girls' gym, flings open the door and calls Angelica over. Angelica is wide-eyed. I'm still holding her diary.

'Is there any good reason,' Lugs asks, 'why this nasty little orc would be raking through your bag?'

I look at Angelica. Save me, I try to say with my eyes.

'No,' she says, and my heart crashes through my boots.

Angelica takes the diary out of my hands. It's still open at the page I was reading. She glances down at the open page, then closes the diary quickly, stuffing it in her bag. 'Except that we're doing a project together for RE. Maybe he was looking for the work we'd done together.'

Lugs stares hard at Angelica. She seems furious at the idea that this might get me off the hook.

'That's right,' I say. 'I had a bang on the head so I was excused PE. I was on my way to the library so I thought I'd do a bit more on the project.'

I guess there are times in your life when you know perfectly well that you are being lied to, but that you can't do anything about it. I can see from the force with which Lugs is compressing her lips together that this is one of those times.

'Angelica, get back in the gym,' Lugs sputters. Angelica skips away. 'And as for you, you objectionable little weasel, you shouldn't be anywhere near here. You have no reason to come anywhere near here and I don't want to see your hideous face within a hundred yards of this place ever again. Do you understand that?'

Well, I suppose if I'm going to do the tango, I think, it may as well be with Lugs as anyone. 'Yes I understand that perfectly. Seeing as I'm a halfway intelligent human being.'

'What did you say?'

'And if I were you I wouldn't go around calling people an orc or a weasel, what with a spectacular pair of listeners like those.'

'How dare you speak to me like that!'

'I mean don't you find them a disadvantage in a high wind?'

'You little —'

All right. I won't tell you the rest. But I get the detention I'm looking for. And a lot more too, but I'd calculated that I can explain to the head that it was Lugs who started the name-calling. Anyway, the point is that I have to spend an hour in after-school detention. And that means that I have a good excuse not to turn up at Café Vienna right after school.

Before the end of the school day I do two things. In full view of Matt I hand Shelly Hobbs a note. The second thing is that I tell Matt to be in Café Vienna after school to sort this nonsense out once and for all.

● ● ● ●

Detention is a yawn. I sit there watching the clock run down. Thing is I told Shelly Hobbs I would be there at four and I'm going to be at least forty-five minutes late.

When I finally roll up at Café Vienna there is no Shelly Hobbs in sight and no sign of Matt either, but Wilko and Tonga are at a table nursing empty glasses. 'You're too late,' Tonga shouts. 'She's been and gone. Your name is mud.'

'Hello, Mud,' says Wilko.

'I'll tell you something else,' says Tonga. 'She's gone off with Matt.'

I join them at the table. 'Lovely,' I say rubbing my hands. 'Shall we all have a glass of fart?'

'Ain't you bothered?' Tonga says suspiciously.

'I told you before: I'm not interested in Shelly. That's why I didn't come at four o'clock.'

'I heard you got detention!' shouts Tonga.

'True.'

'What's going on then?'

'Yeh,' says Wilko, 'what was in that note you gave Shelly?'

'DatingTips.com,' I tell them.

'Eh?'

'Look, boys, when it comes to dating girls everyone needs a wingman. A mate who will take a bullet for a friend. Matt has his eye on Shelly so I thought I'd clear the way for him. Get him and Shelly here at the same time.'

Tonga looks at me doubtfully. 'Are you still going out with Angelica?'

'She's an alien,' I snort back at him.

They laugh at this. 'What's this thing about DatingTips.com?' Wilko asks.

'You should check it out. It's a foolproof way of getting girls. It's all about technique.'

Tonga burps. 'Technique, cobblers.'

But Wilko is interested. 'What do you mean by technique?'

I think for a minute. 'Avoiding things you do that put them off. Doing things that make them interested. But not looking too interested yourself.'

'What things?'

'Body language.'

'Bull,' Tonga says, 'he's just talking bull.'

'You're the same, Tonga. You like Shelly Hobbs just as much as Matt does. But all you do is stare at her bazongas and wipe the drool off your mouth.'

'Bull!'

'It's true, Tonga,' Wilko says. 'You're always leaning in like you want to rest your head on 'em.'

Tonga tries to slap Wilko's ear but he's too slow.

'That's exactly it. Take eye contact. You have to make sure

you're not the one who looks away first.'

'But if you're making eye contact,' Tonga says, 'then that's saying you're interested.'

I have to think about this. I mean, he's right. It is a bit of a contradiction. I think I'll have to go back to DatingTips.com and see what it says about that.

The waitress with the huge thighs appears from the back. She spots me, picks up a menu and heads our way. 'Here,' Wilko says. 'Show us what you mean.'

'No,' I say quickly. 'I don't fancy her so it doesn't count.'

'Go on,' Tonga says. 'If you're so bloody clever.'

She's wearing that short skirt again. As soon as she comes to our table Tonga and Wilko both glance at her thighs and look away. Tonga actually wipes his brow as if the sight of her legs has caused him to sweat. Wilko looks at his fingernails then scratches the back of his neck. If this is body language the pair of them are BELLOWING something or other. I don't know what. Anyway because I'm watching them BEL-LOWING body language I don't look at her thighs. I also make a point of not looking at her eyes.

'Hey,' says the waitress. 'It's Mister Masterful! What are you having?'

I ignore her. In fact I make out that I can see something more interesting through the window of the café. She turns to look. So do Tonga and Wilko. I continue to stare out of the window.

'Well?' she says.

I just gaze out of the window. Now Tonga and Wilko are looking at each other.

Out of the corner of my eye I see the waitress fold her arms and cross her legs at the ankles. 'It's okay,' she says to no one in particular, 'I'm a waitress. I'll just wait.'

Finally I turn slowly towards her, and this time I fix her with deadly eye contact. 'I want one of those caffè lattes that you make so well.'

She stares hard back at me. But I make sure she blinks first. Then she reaches over and grabs my chin between a thumb and forefinger, waggling the bit of loose flesh there. 'God, you could eat him,' she says. Then she goes away to get my order.

Wilko and Tonga are staring at me.

'See?' I say.

• • • •

After leaving Café Vienna we go our separate ways, but not before the waitress blows me a kiss. I mean those fat legs are scary but it shows that I've managed to wind her in. I think I might set up my own website offering dating tips to young guys like myself. Maybe I'll call it DatingTechnique.com. Or perhaps GetaDateForSure.co.uk. I could probably make a load of money.

On the way home I see two figures huddled in a shop doorway in each other's arms. It's Matt and Shelly. Matt spots me and hails me. He darts across the road to intercept me.

Matt puts a hand on my shoulder. 'Thanks, mate,' he says sincerely.

'No problem,' I say.

'*Three things you should know about Matt*,' he says. He's quoting from the note I gave to Shelly. She obviously showed it to him. '*He's a great friend. He's fun company. He's well-poked with cash. He's the second-best looking lad in the school. And though he gets loads of offers he's only got eyes for you.'*

'Well, not all of it's true,' I say.

'Sorry I had you all wrong. I owe you one, Doogie.'

'You do. I took a detention for you. Anyway, Shelly's waiting. See you later.'

He pats me on the arm and nips back across to Shelly. She gives me a little wave.

It's great to see them together. But even that thought doesn't much cheer me up as I walk home alone along the high street, past all the glass-fronted shops. I stop at one glass window and look at my reflection, examining the little wound on the side of my head. I'm worried sick about this thing lying dormant in my brain.

Angelica is probably the only person who can help me and a) she won't even speak to me and b) in her eyes I've made things worse by showing off to Shelly Hobbs and c) Angelica is one of the people who put the thing there in the first place and would probably just as soon slip another chip in there rather than help me and d) Van Helsing just gets me into more and more trouble and e) my parents will completely freak out if I tell them I've got an electronic maggot in my brain and –

I look up again at the reflection of myself in the plate-glass window. My two hands are each grabbing a hunk of my own hair as if I'm trying to pull my brains out by my hair roots. I look ridiculous. And then I start roaring at my own reflection.

'Rrrrrrrrrrrrrrrrrrrrraaaaaaaaaaaaaaaaaaaaaaaaaaagggggghhhhhhhhhhhh!!!

An old lady shuffling along with her shopping stops to look at me. 'We shall get the police on you, we will,' she says.

'You do that,' I say.

'We will,' she says. Then she goes on her way, stopping briefly to check out what's in the windows of the pound shop.

Suddenly I think: you know what? That isn't a bad idea.

I decide to get the police on myself.

19

• • • • • • •

You do the right thing. You behave like a responsible citizen.
I mean, they're always telling you about being responsible. I
get sick of hearing it. I do. All the time they say, well, if you
want your rights and you want to be treated with respect you
have to accept responsibility blah blah blah. Well you do that
and look what happens.

The police station is a modern concrete-and-glass block
set back from the shops. I go in and walk right up to the
counter and there's no one there. There is a bell that you're
supposed to ring.

• • • •

I think about ringing a second time but you can probably get
arrested for that. So I don't. Luckily the desk sergeant
appears, rubbing the corner of his mouth, probably to get rid
of the bacon fat and tomato sauce. He's got dark brown eyes
and he's completely bald. It occurs to me that maybe if you
have to wear a helmet all the time it might make you lose
your hair early. I mean, there are a lot of bald policemen
when you think about it.

He rubs his hands together, like he's going to sell me a
sirloin steak and half a pound of sausage. 'Yes, sir.'

'You'll think I'm mad but it's something I have to tell you.'

He folds his arms and leans on the counter. 'You'd be amazed at what I get to hear, son. Let's have it.'

'Okay. But first, is it like, you know, when you tell a doctor or a priest. You know – confidential?'

'What?'

'When you tell a priest in confession they're not supposed to tell anyone else.'

'Oh, I see. No.'

'No?'

'No it's not like that at all. If it's to do with breaking the law we tell everyone who needs to know.'

'Oh.'

'What's the trouble?'

'Right. Okay. I'm just going to say it straight out, right?'

'Go ahead.'

'Right.'

The desk sergeant blinks at me, waiting. He blinks again. His big brown eyes are on me. 'Take your time.'

'Right.'

Now he stands up straight and rubs his chin. He stares at me. This makes me feels guilty. I don't know why. Maybe it's the uniform.

'I can't say it,' I tell him. 'Sorry. I just can't say it. Maybe I'll come back another day.'

'What's it in connection with?' he asks me.

I try to tell him, but I can't.

'Right,' he says. 'You don't have to say anything. I'll give you a hint and you just nod when we hit the right subject. That way you won't actually have to tell me anything. Right?'

'Okay.'

'Is it to do with taking cars?'

'No.'

'Drugs?'

'No.'

'Breaking into people's houses?'

'No.'

'Setting fire to rubbish bins down Cranmer Street? There's been a lot of that.'

'No.'

'You sure?'

'I'm sure.'

He drums the desk with his fingers, and sticks his tongue in the side of this cheek. 'Can you give me a clue?'

'You'll laugh.'

'No, I won't.'

'Yes, you will.'

'No, I won't.'

'You'll think I'm an idiot.'

'No, I won't.'

'It's about aliens,' I say.

Now he looks at me without blinking. Just stares.

'Extraterrestrials,' I say, in case he doesn't know what I mean by aliens.

He nods seriously and rubs his chin. And just when I think he's going to say something really sarcastic he reaches under the desk and pulls out a big black logbook. 'Let's get the details,' he says. 'Let's start with your name.'

So I tell him everything. I tell him who I am, I tell him about Angelica and her parents, and about Van Helsing.

'Van Helsing?' he says.

'You know him?' I ask.

'Sort of. He's the vampire hunter, isn't he?'

'Is he?'

'Yeh. Hunts vampires. Well, in the story.'

'Did he?'

'Yeh. Good at it, he was.'

'Not aliens?'

'Eh?'

'He didn't hunt aliens, too?'

'Not as far as I know.'

'Who was Holmwood?'

'No idea,' says the desk sergeant. 'Might have been one of Van Helsing's assistants. Can't be certain though.'

Well, I go on to tell him about my first visit to Angelica's house, and about the weird stuff on her dad's computer and about trying to run away and getting caught. I tell him about the chip they put inside my brain while I was unconscious and I show him the scar on the side of my head. He stops making notes to take a look at the scar. Then he makes more notes. We're interrupted briefly when another policeman, much younger, comes in from the street with a rough-looking and unsteady character in a baseball cap.

The desk sergeant stops writing in the book and looks up. 'Oh no, Derek, you haven't done it again, have you?'

'He has,' says the young policeman.

'Oh no, Derek! What are you like?'

The man sways unsteadily. 'Sorry, John. You know. Well. Too bad.'

'Oh Derek. You do disappoint me!' Then he says to the younger policeman. 'Put him in a cell. I'll deal with him after this.'

The man shuffles through to the back as if he knows where

to go. The young policeman follows him.

'What was that about?' I ask the desk sergeant.

'Oh, that's just Derek. So is there anything else?'

I say that's about it and he finishes making his notes. He glances at the clock and makes a note of the time. He asks me to read over what he's written and to sign my name underneath it, which I do. After I've done that he draws two thick lines underneath his report with his biro.

'You won't tell my folks about this, will you? I don't want them to know.'

'Not a word.'

'What will you do?'

'We'll have this investigated.'

'You will?'

'Yep. We'll get someone on to it. Put a watch on their activities. That's all we can do. If anything develops we'll be in touch. Leave it to us.'

'Okay.'

'You can go now, Douglas.'

'Doogie.'

'Okay, you can go now, Doogie.'

'Most people call me Doogie.'

'Right, you can go now, Doogie. Leave it with us.'

'Fair enough.'

'Bye then.'

'Bye. Do I just wait to hear from you?'

'Yep.' He scratches the back of his neck vigorously with the top of his biro.

'See you, then.'

'See you.'

I go out of the door. I get about twenty yards down the

road and then I remember something, so I go back. I don't have to press the bell because the desk sergeant is still there.

'What is it now?' he says.

'You didn't ask me for their address.'

'Whose address?'

'The family I told you about. The Vinterlands. If you're going to put a watch on them you'll need their address.

'You're right. Give me their address.'

I tell him the address and he writes it down. 'Okay,' he says, 'all done.'

I don't bother to say goodbye this time. I don't feel like it. I do feel the desk sergeant's eyes boring into the back of my head as I leave the building.

I get about three hundreds yards down the road, just past the park, before I think: bastard.

• • • •

Me: You got me into this mess! You've got to get me out of it!

Van Helsing: Calm down, Holmwood! Just chill.

Me: Right: stop calling me Holmwood. My name is Doogie, right? Doogie.

Van Helsing: It's a security thing.

Me: Sod that! I don't feel very secure with this microchip stuck in my brain! Doogie Doogie Doogie! DOOGIE. I don't care who is monitoring this. MY NAME IS DOOGIE!

Van Helsing: Okay, okay. Doogie.

Me: So what are you going to do?

Van Helsing: I'm working on it.

Me: I don't believe you! You've done nothing! And I'm the one with an alien hornet's egg planted in my brain while you DO NOTHING!

Van Helsing:

Me: Are you there?

Van Helsing:

Me: Are you there?

Van Helsing: Yes, I'm here.

Me: I went to the police today.

Van Helsing: You did what?

Me: Police. In town. I went and told them everything.

Van Helsing: Stupid. That was very stupid.

Me: What else am I supposed to do about this maggot fattening in my brain? Who else can I tell?

Van Helsing: No. I don't think you would do that, Doogie. Even if you did they wouldn't believe you. They'd laugh at you.

Me: Well I did and they didn't.

Van Helsing: Didn't what?

Me: Laugh.

Van Helsing: You actually went there?

Me: Yes.

Van Helsing: Fool! Did you tell them about me?

Me: I told them what I told them.

Van Helsing: DID YOU TELL THEM ABOUT ME????

Me:

Van Helsing: WELL???????? DID YOU??????

Me: No.

Van Helsing: You're an idiot. I've a good mind to log off and never communicate with you again.

Me: If you did that then I would tell the police about you.

Van Helsing: You little idiot!

Me: You seem more worried about that than about this wasp's nest in my skull, you bastard!

Van Helsing: This is getting us nowhere.

Me: Well, do something! I need some help!

Van Helsing: Hasn't it occurred to you that the policeman you spoke to may well be one of them??? I've told you before that they target the police, government and the medical profession. That's their plan!

Me: I don't care about them. I just want this chip thing out of my brain. You said that someone in your group knows how to take it out! Get them to do it.

Van Helsing: It's not that easy. The person I was referring to lives in California. There are more incidents of this type in California.

Me: California!

Van Helsing: Yes, in the USA.

Me: I know where California is!!!!!!

Van Helsing: Look, if you promise to stay calm and not do anything else stupid I'll see what advice I can get. We'll take care of it.

Me: You'd better. If you don't I'll go back to the police and tell them you groomed me through the Internet.

Van Helsing: Groomed? I did no such thing. And I don't take kindly to threats.

Me: Just do it!

I log off. I'm really angry that Van Helsing doesn't take me seriously. Really angry.

● ● ●●

At tea that evening Mum waits until Dad has finished and then she asks me to stack the dishwasher for her.

'Is everything all right at school, our Doogie?'

'Yes.'

'Only you look so worried about things these days. Like something's on your mind.'

'No. Nothing's on my mind.' Only an electronic scorpion's egg about to hatch, that's all, Mum.

'How's Angelica? Are you still seeing her?'

'No. It's off.'

'Ahhhhh,' she says. 'I see. Want to talk it about it with your mum?'

I look round me, as if she's talking about some other mum. I mean does she really think I might want to talk about it with her? She can't possibly think that. If she does she's even thicker than I suspected, and that is pretty damned thick. 'No, Mum.'

'I understand, our Doogie. I really do.'

I stick my head as far in the dishwasher as I can so that she can't see me blush. The cheese grater is to hand. I'd rather use it to scrape the skin off my buttocks than talk about a girlfriend with my mum.

'Well, I'm here if you want to talk, our Doogie. Mums aren't just here for making the dinner, you know.'

'Frrrgggggagaggagaaaashanana,' I say from inside the dishwasher.

'What's that, our Doogie?'

'Thanks, right. I'll just go upstairs. To my room. Got some school homework to get done.'

19

I'm not sure that everything I read at DatingTips.com is right. For example, it says that if you show no interest in a girl then she'll be mad for you. Well that's not true for Angelica. I'm showing no interest in her and she's showing no interest back. She's just looking at me as if I'm a bit sad.

Later that day I decide I'm going to tell Matt. I have to. He's the one out of all my friends who is the most sensible. It happens during Science in period three, when Pinky is busy with setting up an experiment involving the dissection of a locust. He gives me the lead in.

'So are you still going out with Angelica, or what?'

'Or what.'

'Is that a no? I was thinking we could make a foursome. You and her, me and Shelly.'

'See this scar?'

'What about it?'

'She waited until I was asleep then she slipped a microchip in.'

'What, you slept together?'

'Never mind that. Did you hear what I said?'

'Yes – you said you slept together. Wow!'

'I didn't say that at all, you drong. I said she slipped a

microchip in my head. But you were too fixed on your own dirty thoughts.'

'Funny!'

Pinky overhears us. 'What's going on? You boys are gossiping like a pair of old ladies.'

'It's the locusts. They smell funny.'

They do too. It's the formaldehyde. I don't like the smell or the look of them. I wonder if they look anything like the thing that's about to be born inside my skull.

I give up trying to explain it all to Matt. What's the point? He's too hypnotised by Shelly Hobbs's bazongas to pay attention to what I'm trying to tell him.

• • • •

'Hey, our Doogie,' Mum says that evening, while I'm watching *The Weakest Link* on telly, 'you've become a proper moper.'

'Eh?'

'You. Moping around the place.'

'Eh?'

'You've a face as long as a gasman's mac.'

'We don't have gasmen to read the meter any more, Mum.'

'Yes we do.'

'No we don't – you fill in the numbers on a card now.'

'They still come round. Anyway that's not what we're talking about.'

'Yes it is. You said my face was –'

'That's not what we're talking about at all. Don't be funny.'

'I'm not being funny.'

'Yes you are, you're being funny.'

'No, I'm not.'

'Have you actually called her?'

'Eh?'

'Stop saying eh? You know what I'm talking about.'

'I'm trying to watch the telly!'

'Have you actually just called her and tried to smooth things out?'

'Eh?'

'*Doogie!*'

'What are you on about?'

'I'm talking about Angelica, of course. Have you actually tried talking to her?'

I don't know how this happens. But my face erupts for no reason into a steaming froth of weird pinkness. A prickly heat starts at my neck and rushes up over my ears and explodes like spitting volcanic lava out of the top of my head, and it comes out like this: 'SHADDUP! SHADDUP! SHADDUP!'

I leap out of my chair and race out of the room, slamming the door behind me and thumping up the stairs. I hear Mum go, 'Ooooo, our Doogie!' as I bang shut the bedroom door behind me and shove my computer chair against it to stop anyone coming in.

2O
· · · · · · · ·

Van Helsing: I'm prepared to do it myself.

   Me: What? Do what?

Van Helsing: Remove it.

   Me: ?

Van Helsing: I've been in touch with our colleague in California. Let's call her April. There is no way April can come to England right now. I offered to pay her flight over here so she could help us out. But she's too tied up with things.

   Me: And?

Van Helsing: She's given me very detailed and careful instructions about how to remove it for you.

   Me: My God! What does it involve?

Van Helsing: Let's not go into that right now.

   Me: Oh sure! You don't want to tell me! Perhaps it involves slicing the top of my head off with a chain saw! Like with a soft-boiled egg and –

Van Helsing: Holmwood . . . I mean Doogie.

   Me: Maybe you reach inside with one of those clicky things, yes, an ice-cream scoop or –

Van Helsing: Doogie.

   Me: Or maybe you just use an ordinary power tool with a sixteenth-inch drill-bit or –

Van Helsing: DOOGIE!

Me: Or how about a super-powerful magnet that just rips the thing out of the side of my –

Van Helsing: FOR GOD'S SAKE DOOGIE CALM YOURSELF!

Me: You have to tell me what's involved!

Van Helsing: It's a surprisingly simple process.

Me: How simple?

Van Helsing: I will apply a local anaesthetic to the existing wound area to freeze the skin. I'll re-open the wound with a scalpel. A tiny incision. The chip is near the surface. Then I cauterise a simple tool fashioned into a loop from copper wire to hook the chip out. April says that so long as the tissue hasn't begun to absorb the chip, it should come out very easily.

Me: And if it has? Absorbed it.

Van Helsing: April has given me more complex directions to cover that eventuality. We'll cross that bridge if we come to it. As it is, you won't feel a thing. Not much anyway.

Me: When?

Van Helsing: Tomorrow.

Me: You're joking!

Van Helsing: The longer we leave it, the more the brain tissue will have absorbed the chip.

Me: All right, all right. I'm just a bit shaken up, that's all. When?

Van Helsing: Two in the afternoon.

Me: That's no good, I'm in school!

Van Helsing: It's the only time I have. Look, I'm making a lot of sacrifices in order to do this for you. I expect some willingness in return.

· 175 ·

Me: But how am I supposed to get out of lessons?

Van Helsing: You'll think of something.

Me: Thanks a lot. Where are we going to do it?

Van Helsing: In my car.

Me: What? I'm not getting in your car! I've no idea who you are. You could be a perv for all I know!

Van Helsing: You're going to let me root around in your brain for a microchip but you won't get in my car??? Are you insane?

Me: I'm not getting in your car. That's final.

Van Helsing: Where do you suggest? The market-place? The middle of the theatre? We need to be very discreet, Doogie. Very very discreet. We can't afford to be seen doing this.

Me: I know somewhere. There's this café and it has booths. It's private enough. We could meet there.

Van Helsing: Booths? I don't like the sound of it. We might be interrupted.

Me: It's called Café Vienna.

Van Helsing: All right. We'll meet there at least. But if I don't like the look of things we'll have to go from there back to my car and drive somewhere else. Where is this Café Vienna?

● ● ● ●

Next day at school I make up an emergency dental appointment for the afternoon so that I can bunk off school and meet Van Helsing. I tell the school office that the only time the dentist could fit me in is during school hours. To make it look convincing I have to go round wincing and twitching and pretending to massage my jaw. Perhaps I do it a bit too much because Pinky, who is a sarcastic bastard, sees me pulling faces and goes, 'Toothache, Doogie? Or just the normal agony and ecstasy of teenage life?'

Of course I have no idea what Van Helsing looks like. I don't know if he's young or old, short or tall, black or white, fat or thin, dumpy or pointy. I forgot to ask for a description. For all I know, Van Helsing might be female. Imagine that. You meet someone on the Internet and you've no idea what you're getting.

I do start to wonder if he's a perv. He seemed very keen to get me in the car. But then again, as I think back, he's never said anything pervy or made any weird suggestions. And it is me who is forcing us to meet face-to-face, after all.

The morning is a nightmare because all I can think about is meeting Van Helsing. I'm nervous enough about meeting him without the thought of what he's going to do to pull the microchip out of my skull. At break time I have to go into the boys' toilets to throw up. Afterwards I wash my face and try some breathing exercises to calm down, but it just gets me funny looks from boys coming into the toilets.

When I go outside for some fresh air I happen to walk past Angelica.

'You all right?' she asks.

'Yeh. Fine. Completely fine. Why wouldn't I be?'

'You look a bit pale, that's all.'

'Pale? Yeh, well when you've got what's in my head you would look pale, wouldn't you?'

'No one can ever work out what's in your head.'

'Oh I think you've got a pretty good idea.'

'Is that supposed to be a compliment?'

She's playing games of course. She knows that I know. But she's not going to let on. Never going to come out and admit to what they did to me while I was unconscious. But she is happy to taunt me with it. Happy to talk about it without actually talking about it. Right. Two can play at that game.

'You can take it how you like.'

'All right. I'll take it as a compliment that I know what's in your head.'

'Yep. You're the only person who knows what's in my head.'

'Surely not the only person.'

'Whatever. I won't be here this afternoon. I'm going to have it taken out.'

She blinks. 'You are?'

'Yes. This afternoon.'

'Oh right. I overheard you telling Pinky you were going to the dentist. Hope it's not too painful.'

I look at her closely. Is that a threat? Is she saying that something might go wrong? The trouble is her eyes don't give her away. 'I'm getting pretty used to anaesthetics,' I say meaningfully.

'Yes. I suppose you are.'

I'm already walking away when I tell her, 'Anyway, I'll return your property.'

She just stares after me.

● ● ● ●

I miss lunch because I still feel like throwing up. I walk out of school and take a bus to Café Vienna. I'm about ten minutes early for my appointment with Van Helsing. I think about hanging around outside the café until Van Helsing arrives. If I don't like the look of him I won't go in. But it's pretty nippy outside and anyone loitering around in school uniform will eventually attract the attention of the police, so I decide to go in.

There are a few people in there already. Two construction workers in luminous visibility jackets are drinking tea and reading newspapers. A lovey-dovey couple holding hands look like they've escaped from an office for some romance. There's a little old lady with white hair, talking to herself as she sorts through her shopping bags. And one other table is taken up by three Asian businessmen sharing a joke about something.

In other words, no Van Helsing yet. He told me he would be alone.

'Hiya, what you doing off school?' It's Thunderthighs, taking an order from the romantic couple. She sings this to me in a loud voice so that everyone in the café looks up at me. Thanks, I think. 'Have a seat and I'll be with you in a moment.'

I slip into one of the booths at the back. I feel hot and then I feel chilled. My heart is pounding and I know I'm sweating because my lips taste salty. I loosen my school tie and try to stay calm. My appointment with Van Helsing is scheduled for two o'clock and like I say, I'm about ten minutes early.

Thunderthighs startles me by swinging open the doors of the booth. 'Bunking off school, is it?'

'Dental appointment,' I lie easily. 'Bit early. Thought I'd have a coffee.'

'One coffee. Latte? Americano?'

'Normal. And a glass of water please. Big glass.'

'You all right? You look terribly pale.'

'I'm meeting my uncle,' I croak.

'You might be meeting your uncle, but you still look pale.

Do you want an aspirin with your coffee?' She leans over and places the flat of her palm against my forehead. Her pudgy fingers feel cool. 'You should get your mum to tuck you into bed.'

'Dentist's,' I say. 'Got to go. Tooth.'

She looks at me doubtfully before turning on her heel. After a minute she returns with the coffee, a glass of water and two white tablets, which she leaves on the table. 'It's only paracetamol. I'm not supposed to give you them but you look a bit rough.'

I take the headache pills and glug the water.

While I'm waiting for Van Helsing to arrive I suddenly have a nightmarish thought: what if I know him already? What if, for example, it turns out to be someone I've met while working at the builders' yard? What if it's a local shop-keeper, say, or the postman? What if it's one of my school-teachers? Or the headmaster?

At two o'clock exactly, the person I take to be Van Helsing appears at the door.

● ● ● ●

I know it's him. I don't know how I know: I just know. The odd thing is that there is nothing at all odd about him. He's as normal as they come. He looks like a salesman — the type who drives up and down the country in a Ford Mondeo with product samples in the boot of his car. He's wearing an untidy dark suit with a light blue shirt and he carries a laptop computer bag across his shoulder. He stands in the doorway, scanning the customers.

I stand up and look across the top of the chin-high swing doors to the booth. Our eyes meet.

He nods. I nod back at him.

He walks briskly through the café, shouldering his computer bag. He pushes open the swing doors to the booth and sits down. 'Holmwood, I presume?'

'Doogie,' I say. I try to sound firm, but my voice wobbles a bit.

'Have it your way.'

He unzips his bag and takes out a laptop computer, which he flips open and powers up. While he's doing this I have a chance to look hard at him. He's balding, but with thick hair behind and above his ears and with wisps of hair coiled across the top of his freckled head. He has large, rather sweaty hands. There's a signet ring on the index finger of his right hand which he fiddles with while he's waiting for the computer to power up. His eyes are a surprising blue I associate with honesty. I notice a bead of sweat on his upper lip and it occurs to me that he might be just as nervous as I am.

'I'm going to show you something you won't see on YouTube,' he says.

He strokes a few keys and then rotates the laptop so that I can see the screen.

It's a bit of film. There's no sound. There's just the head of a young woman blinking at the camera. A hand is dabbing the side of her head with cotton wool. Then something is shaken from a bottle on to the cotton wool and applied again to the young woman's head.

'My friend in California emailed this for you,' says Van Helsing, 'so that you can see how simple the process is.'

The film is crudely put together. The picture fades and now there's the same young woman blinking at the camera but now she holds a handwritten card saying 'FIFTEEN

MINUTES LATER'. I don't see what happens next because the booth doors swing open and Thunderthighs appears.

'Hello, uncle,' she says cheerily, 'what can I get you?'

Van Helsing slams the computer shut. It only makes her look at him oddly. 'Do you have cranberry juice?' he asks her and I notice he doesn't look her in the eye.

'We do.'

'One cranberry juice.' Still he looks away from her.

'Anything else for you?' she says to me.

I shake my head. She makes eyes at me, as if to say *what's wrong with him?* I ignore her. She goes away.

'I really want to be out of here very fast,' he says. 'What you were just watching was the application of a local anaesthetic.' He reaches into his jacket inside pocket and produces a small bottle and some cotton wool. 'We should get on with this at once because we have to wait for it to take effect.'

Van Helsing whips the cap off the bottle and shakes some of its contents on to the cotton wool. It smells very strong, like felt-tip pens. 'Lean forward.'

'Eh?'

'Lean forward. Unless you want to apply it yourself.'

I think I would rather put it on myself, but I let him do it. I tilt my head towards him and he starts dabbing the scar on my temple and the skin around the scar with the cotton wool. He rubs it in small circles. After a while the skin starts to feel a bit sore and I tell him to stop.

He shrugs and flips open the computer again. He points the cursor at play. 'Ready?'

The young woman in the film lifts her hair back to reveal a small scar. It's not quite in the same place as where mine is, but it's fairly close. It's also a rather bigger scar than mine.

Then a hand reaches across, holding some surgical tool. Maybe it's a scalpel like the one we used to dissect the locusts in science class. I don't know. Anyway, the person holding the tool makes a small cut where the old scar is. I wince a bit. I want to go *ouch!* But there is no blood. None at all.

Then the scene fades to black and then fades up again. Now the hand has a loop of, like, copper wire, which gets poked in around the wound. It makes me want to faint but the young woman is staring at the camera with a blank expression, even the start of a smile sometimes. Obviously she can't feel anything.

The film jumps a bit and then the hand pulls something out on the loop of copper wire.

A close-up shows it to be a microchip. It looks a tiny bit like a SIM card for a mobile phone. But a lot smaller and made up of fine wire filaments.

Then the scene fades out and the film stops. That's it.

I lean back.

'Simple,' says Van Helsing, spinning the computer round and shutting it all down.

'Simple? You call that simple?' I nearly shout.

'You can leave it in if you want,' he says. 'Just say the word and I'm out of here.'

I blow out my cheeks. I don't like it at all, but the alternative of leaving the chip inside my head seems worse. I mean it really is like going to the dentist and getting a tooth out, isn't it? Half an hour of agony to save years of pain and who knows what? I have no choice.

'Are you ready to come to the car?' says Van Helsing.

'How long will it take?'

'Just a few minutes.'

'I'd rather stay here.'

'I don't like it. What if we're interrupted?'

'We won't be. You can't see into the booth unless you open the doors to come in. Maybe you should get on with it.'

'We need a few more minutes for the anaesthetic to kick in properly. Is it working?'

I rub my head. It's already pretty numb and it feels like someone else's hand is tickling it.

He reaches inside his computer bag and he pulls out a plastic box. When he opens it I see the scalpel – and it is identical to the one I used in the school lab – and another piece of plastic with copper wire attached. I don't know what I expected but it all looks a bit primitive to me.

'You just going to fish around with that thing?'

'My friend from California says it's very easy.'

I rub the scar, feeling the bone beneath and I suddenly have a thought. 'What about the skull? How you going to get past my skull?'

He blinks at me. 'We go through the same hole they made when they put the thing in.'

'Oh.'

Van Helsing's cranberry juice arrives and he snaps shut the box containing the two tools. Thunderthighs notices this. She places his glass of juice on the table in silence. Her nose twitches. I think she can smell the anaesthetic.

Then she looks at me. 'Are you sure you're all right?' I nod at her rather weakly. She looks at Van Helsing, who still refuses to meet her eyes. 'He was feeling a bit poorly earlier,' she says to him.

'Yes,' Van Helsing says. 'He's been a bit under the weather.' He still won't make eye contact. He needs to. I'm willing him to, but he won't.

Now she looks back at me. This time she gives a little quizzical shake of her head. 'You sure I can't get you anything?'

I know what she's saying to me. She's saying: *is everything all right here?* She's saying: *what's going on?* She's saying: *who is this weird guy?* And I do want to say: *help, get me out of this situation, get this chip out of my brain, take me home to Mum and Dad* but of course I can't. And even though I'm ashamed to admit it I'm really close to tears. But I stop myself cos I have no choice but to go through with it.

'No. I'm fine, thanks,' I say.

Thunderthighs shakes her head and leaves us to it.

'Eye contact,' I say to him after she's gone.

'You what?'

'Eye contact. You should make eye contact. Everyone knows that. Even when you're not trying to date someone; though if you are you should especially make eye contact because it says that on DatingTips.com. Because if you don't it looks weird.'

He doesn't respond to this. Instead he opens the box again and takes out the stainless steel scalpel. It has a plastic cover. He removes it. The blade looks scary and sharp.

'She knows something is up. That's because of your weird behaviour.'

'No it's not,' he says, cleaning the blade with an antiseptic wipe. 'Come on, let's get on with it. You're making me nervous.'

'I'm telling you she knows something is going on!'

'Of course she does.'

'Eh? Why would she?'

'Because she's one of them.'

I sit back. My mouth falls open. 'Eh?'

'The waitress,' he repeats, 'is one of *them*.'

'You're joking.'

He looks up from cleaning the blade of the scalpel. He says nothing.

'But I know her. The waitress. I've known her a while, I mean.'

'Like you know Angelica?'

I get up and peer across the top of the swing doors enclosing the booth. The waitress – Thunderthighs – is at the far end of the café and she's talking to the chef, a big guy in kitchen whites. They're both looking my way. I sit down quickly. 'I'm amazed,' I say.

'I checked this place out yesterday at the same time. I recognised her as one of them from certain tell-tale signs. After a while they become very easy to spot.'

'I can hardly believe it. I'd never have known.'

'Yesterday when I came by this place was completely empty. Why do you think it's so busy now?'

'What do you mean?'

'See those two men disguised as construction workers? What's wrong with them?'

I get up and look at them again. The two guys with hard hats and luminous jackets are still reading newspapers. 'Nothing that I can see.'

'Look at their shoes.'

I look at their shoes under the table. I don't see anything unusual and I say so. Then one of the construction workers sees me staring at them, so I sit down again.

'Construction workers wear safety boots for building

sites. They're both wearing casual shoes, like you might wear in an office. These are the sort of things they get wrong all the time.'

'But what if —'

'If what, Doogie?'

I let out a big sigh.

'And have you looked at those Asian businessmen?'

'What, them too?'

'They are Sikhs. As you can tell by the turban that one of them is wearing. Yet they're all eating meat. Most Sikhs are vegetarians.'

'But maybe they're just —'

'Maybe they're just what, Doogie?'

'It's incredible.'

'Don't believe me? Why not ask your waitress friend. But she's the one who got them to come here. They know we're doing something. They just don't know what.'

'But they were already here before me.'

'You must have blabbed to someone. Can you think of anyone you might have blabbed to?'

I cradle my head in my hands. Of course, I told Angelica earlier on! I even told her I was going to have the thing taken out! She knew I wasn't going to the dentist. She must have figured out that I would come here. I can't believe that I was so stupid!

'You see why I told you security is paramount, Doogie? Are you prepared to listen to me now?'

I stand up and look at the other people in the café. 'What about the lovey-dovey couple?'

'Them too, I'm afraid.'

'And the little old lady?'

'She's talking away, pretending to be eccentric. Very convenient, eh Doogie? Look at her closely. She has an ear-piece.'

I look him in the eye. He nods. Then I look back at the old lady. She looks hard at me. Suddenly she has a cruel look. She touches her ear-piece. I can see she's getting messages through it. They're everywhere. Suddenly I feel very scared. 'They have us trapped!' I say.

'Don't panic. There's a door at the back. If we get up and go quickly, we can get to my car and they won't be able to stop us.' The sweat is pouring off me. The Sikh businessmen. The construction workers. The lovers. The little old lady. The waitress and the chef. They're all pretending to look away. Only the old lady is looking, and I sense that they're getting messages from her.

'We're running out of time, Doogie,' says Van Helsing.

The sweat is pouring from me now. I glance round at the back door. It might work. We could catch them by surprise and make a sudden run for it. I gulp some water.

'Ready, Doogie?'

I nod. I grab the sides of the table, so that I can spring to my feet on a given signal. I can taste the paracetamol in my mouth.

Wait a minute, I think. *Wait a minute.*

I look again at the little old lady. She does have an ear-piece. But it just looks like a normal hearing-aid to me. And she is chattering away but she's talking to herself. Then I look at the Sikh businessmen and I remember that my mate Wilko is a Sikh but he's not strict about it and he eats meat all the time. I look at the construction workers' shoes. I look at Thunderthighs, laying places at the tables now that the chef has gone back in the kitchen.

'Hang on a minute,' I whisper. 'You're making out that every single person in this café is an alien?'

He nods.

'All of them?'

'All of them.'

'You're a raving lunatic!'

'Oh dear,' says Van Helsing, rising from his seat. 'I'm too late.'

'Too late? What do you mean too late?'

'They got to you, didn't they, Doogie?'

'Got to me? What you on about?'

'The chip has already started working.'

'Eh?'

He lifts the scalpel in his hand. 'Come on Doogie. There may still be time after all. Let me take it out.'

I suddenly see a demented gleam in his eye. He waves the scalpel in the air, just two feet away from my face. 'You're bloody barmy!' I shout. 'Completely bloody barmy!'

'Don't let them win you over, Doogie,' he hisses, leaning in with the blade.

'Help!' I shout. 'Help!' I dance out of his reach and smack the booth doors wide open, running up and away between the tables. Everyone stops talking. The businessmen look up at me open-mouthed. The lovers tighten their grip on each other's hands. One of the construction workers is on his feet. Even the little old lady has stopped muttering to herself. Thunderthighs stops laying tables and comes rushing up to me.

But Van Helsing is already on his way out, clutching his computer. He keeps his head down and his eyes averted from everyone in the café, including me. Within seconds he's out of the café and away down the street.

The chef appears clutching a huge machete. It's still got

bits of meat and blood on it.

'You all right?' shouts Thunderthighs, grasping me by the arm.

I'm looking at the door, which is closing behind Van Helsing, and I'm massaging my brow where he rubbed the anaesthetic. I'm thinking what might have happened if he'd gone ahead. 'Yeh. Yeh. I'm fine.'

'Who is he?' says Thunder Thighs.

'He's a nutcase,' I say.

The chef waves his machete. 'Want me to go after him?'

'No. No, it's okay.'

'He isn't your uncle at all, is he?' says Thunderthighs. 'How well do you know him?'

'Not at all, really. I met him on the Internet.'

'Met him on the Internet?' shouts the chef. 'You don't meet people from the Internet! Everybody knows that.'

Then everyone in the café is muttering the word Internet. The businessmen, the construction workers, the lovers are all talking across the tables to each other, agreeing with each other about the stupidity of meeting someone on the Internet. Only the little old lady stays out of this conversation, like she's missed all of it.

'You're shaking,' says Thunderthighs. 'Come on. Sit down and I'll bring you a drink.'

She wants to lead me to a table, but I need to get back to school before the end of the last lesson. I know I'll make it if I leave now. I thank her and pay for the drinks. She lets me off having to pay for the cranberry juice. Everyone watches me leave.

I walk down the street towards the bus stop, stroking the tiny scar on my right temple.

21

● ● ● ● ● ● ● ●

I get back to school with about ten minutes to spare and even though it's pretty pointless I take my seat. It's Religious Studies, so I haven't missed anything.

I sit there thinking what a narrow escape I've just had. I was *that* close to letting Van Helsing loose with his scalpel and I wonder what would have happened if he'd unzipped my skull. The amazing thing is that up until the last moment he seemed so sane. He's always seemed sane. Maybe it's the sane-seeming ones you have to watch in this world.

I wonder if everyone in Van Helsing's world is an alien. I guess that's how it works: as soon as I didn't want to go along with his plan, he decided I was an alien too. I look over at Angelica at her desk. She's writing away. At this moment she doesn't seem alien at all. She just looks like a pretty girl writing in class. But that doesn't mean she isn't one. It still doesn't mean that I'm wrong about her. I mean, Van Helsing may be completely insane, but that doesn't mean there is no such thing as an alien, does it? Maybe Van Helsing started out like me. Maybe he had an experience with a girlfriend and it drove him crazy. Perhaps that's when he started seeing aliens everywhere he looked.

I've been an idiot to let myself be won over by someone

I'd never even met. Someone on the Internet. As I look back over events, most of my troubles can be put down to Van Helsing's original mad scheme to get me poking around inside Angelica's house. I think there must be loads of Van Helsings lurking out there in the shadows of the Internet, ready to direct kids over the cliff edge. Gang leaders. Drug dealers. Politicians. Religious nutcases. All going: here, kiddies, here's some sweeties for you, follow me.

I feel such a prat for falling for it.

After the lesson is over and I'm getting ready to go home, the late-afternoon sun flares though the glass windows of the school corridor, making everything turn peaches and red. Into this crazy light walks Angelica. I feel a fist in my gut as she walks by. I try a smile.

She doesn't smile back. But she stops. 'How did it go?' she asks me.

'Okay.'

'You look a bit shaken up.'

I shrug.

'Which one was it?' she asks me.

I realise she's talking about my tooth. I look her in the eye. I think she means it. I remember to nurse my jaw. 'One at the back.'

She shivers. 'I hate the dentist's. All that shiny steel equipment.'

'Yeh,' I say, 'I know what you mean.'

Then she leans forward suddenly, and her hand flies up to her face. She touches her eyeball with her fingertips, and there, right in front of me, I think she's going to remove her cyborg eye all over again.

'What are you doing?' I shout in horror. Even though I

know this will confirm everything I thought about her, I don't want it to happen.

'It's okay,' she says, 'I've got it.'

She looks at her hand and then she blinks at me, and it's almost a relief to see she hasn't actually pulled her cyborg eye out of her socket this time.

'Got what? What have you got?'

'My contact lens,' she says. And she holds it out for me to see, and there, on the pink pad of her fingertip, is the small round glassy disc of her contact lens. The crimson light flooding in through the windows dances on the lens for a moment; and I wonder if that's what I really saw when I thought she'd removed her eye on the bus that day.

My mouth hangs open. My heart is hammering. I can't speak.

'Oh well,' Angelica says. 'See you.'

She turns and walks down the school corridor. I want to shout after her, tell her to wait for me, that we could walk home together, that I think I've been a complete tosser. But I don't. I just go, 'See you.'

I wait until long after she's gone. Then I drag myself down the corridor. I give myself a good hard punch on the jaw. 'You tosser, Doogie,' I hiss at myself. Then I punch myself with my other hand, on the other side of my jaw. 'You idiot! You tosser!' I go to punch myself for a third time, but I notice two little kids from Year Seven trying to pass me in the corridor. They practically squeeze themselves up against the wall to get by.

They make no eye contact.

• • • •

Tea that evening is my favourite: toad-in-the-hole with mash and onion gravy. Mum makes it once a week for me specially. But I can't face it. I pick at it. I push it around the plate. Dad's tucking into his sausage and mash and telling us about a scaffolder at work who fell thirty feet and only winded himself. Mum is pretending to listen but really she's watching me.

I get up and tell them I'm going to my room to do some homework.

'No pudding?' says Dad.

'No appetite today,' I tell him.

'No dinner and no pudding? You won't be any good to Chalky on Saturday if you don't eat!'

'Leave him,' Mum says.

I go up the stairs. I hear Dad say, 'What's up with him, then?'

In my room I power up my computer and then I switch it off again. There's one person in particular I don't want to be hearing from. I won't be visiting Van Helsing's chatroom in a hurry.

I wish I could message Angelica, though. I fiddle with the text on my phone, composing messages that I don't send. Firstly, DatingTips.com says that the best way to get someone back is to ignore them completely. And secondly, I couldn't stand the rejection if I didn't get an answer.

I lie on my bed staring at the ceiling, feeling miserable and stuck.

After a while I hear a tap on the door. It's Mum.

'Can I come in?' she says, coming in.

She sits on the side of my bed and starts fiddling with the laces on my shoes. 'How many times, our Doogie? Shoes off when on the bed. Shoes off.' She pulls my shoes off and squeezes my foot. 'Tell your mum then, our Doogie.'

'Eh?'

'That's what mums are for you know.'

'What?'

'A problem shared is a problem halved.'

'Eh?'

'Shouldn't keep it all bottled up, you know.'

'Huh?'

'Tell me what's on your mind!'

'Eh? What? Nothing! Nothing's on my mind. Nothing at all. I don't go around with things on my mind.'

'Doogie!'

She's not buying it. This is awful. She's come here to have a heart-to-heart. My mum is so thick she can't even see that having a heart-to-heart with your mum is worse than . . . worse than having your head slit open by a scalpel-wielding lunatic who thinks everyone on earth but him is an alien. Much worse. I make to sit up but she presses her hand against my chest to push me back down. She's surprisingly strong, too.

'Doogie, I can't stand to see you going round like this. You've been terrible the last few days. You're pale. You look sick. Your head is down, your shoulders are slumped, you shamble about the place muttering to yourself.'

'I'm not that bad!'

'Yes you are! You are. I'm not stupid, Doogie. I know what it's all about. Have you and Angelica had words?'

'Had words? Well you have words as soon as you say hello, don't you?'

'Don't be funny with me, Doogie. I'm not offering my help so that you can make a fool of me.'

There's a warning in her voice. This is a side of Mum I don't see very often. 'Soz. I mean sorry.'

'Are you not seeing each other any more?'

'No.'

'Would you like to see her?'

I nod.

'And does she not want to see you?'

'I don't know, Mum. I don't know.'

'Well, that's a start. If you don't know, it means she might. Have you asked her if you can make it up?'

'No.'

'Doogie! Why ever not?'

'Well . . . the best way to get someone back is to make out you're not bothered.'

'Who on earth has told you *that*, our Doogie?'

I'm not about to tell her I've been researching dating techniques on the Internet, am I? So I just say, 'Some lad at school.'

'Well, when you see this lad again you tell him he's an idiot. I've never heard such tripe. The only person who would come running to you because you ignore them is the kind of person so needy you wouldn't want to be bothered with them anyway!'

I think about this. Maybe my mum is not so thick after all.

'Why can't you just phone her?'

'Cos I don't know what's going on in her head.'

'It isn't a head game. It's here you feel things.' She puts her hand on the flat of her belly. 'Phone her.'

'It's not that simple. I made a mistake with her. And now I can't really look her in the eye.'

'What kind of mistake?'

I let out a big sigh and shake my head. I'm not getting into it with my mum. No way.

Mum nods. 'All right, you don't have to tell me what kind of mistake. But listen to this: the person who never makes a mistake never makes anything. I had a good look at Angelica when she came round, and she seemed to me a good sort. So why don't you just approach her – say you're sorry you made a mistake and ask her to give you another chance. It's as simple as that.'

I groan and hold my head in my hands.

Mum gets up from the bed. 'Listen, my darling: if you want sand on the back of your lorry,' she says, 'then you've got to put your spade into the sand.'

Mum leaves my room and closes the door quietly behind her.

I lie on my bed thinking, *eh?*

• • • •

Next day in school I watch Angelica closely. I want to talk to her but she's never on her own and I'm certainly not going to make a public exhibition of myself. I almost get a chance after the second lesson, but I blow it. Then I see her alone briefly at break time, but I dither and she's soon joined by two other girls.

Finally at lunchtime I see her in the cloakroom, sorting books in her bag. Matt, Tonka and Wilko are bellowing in my ear about playing footie in the school yard, but I make my way over to her instead. She's absorbed in what she's doing. I'm either going to have to hover behind her until she turns round or I'm going to have to tap her on the shoulder. I tap.

She jumps. She's so startled her bag falls to the floor.

'Sorry. Didn't mean to . . .'

'To what?' she says sharply, stooping to collect her books.

I think, *this is already not going well; time to withdraw.*

Anyway I decide to say my piece. I take a deep breath. My lips suddenly feel like they've swollen to twice their normal size. My gob feels like it's full of cement and my tongue sticks to the roof of my mouth. I go to say *I'm sorry I've been an idiot* but what comes out is, 'Ham swordfish five beans an Indian did it.'

'Pardon?' she says.

Aggh! I can't believe what's happening! For some reason the power of speech had been taken away from me at the crucial moment! My face is on fire! My ears are burning red! I can feel my cheeks flaming! A thousand fire-ants crawl across my scalp and I want to grab my hair and pull it out by the roots and run away!

I blink at her. She blinks back at me, shaking her head slightly. 'I didn't catch what you said,' she says.

'No. Me neither!'

Now she looks at me like I'm completely crazy. For a moment she looks worried. How can it all be coming out so wrong?

'I'm sorry,' I try again. 'I've been an idiot.'

'And?'

'I wondered if you'd give me another chance.'

'Why would I do that?'

I take a deep breath. 'Not going to make this easy for me, are you?'

'Why should I?'

'Anyone can make a mistake.' I hear my mum's voice at the back of me. 'The person who never makes a mistake never makes anything.'

'So what are you trying to make?'

'It up.'

'What?'

'Make it up. To you. I'm trying to make it up to you.'

'Hmmm. Keep going.'

'How about we meet. Café Vienna. Oh heck not there. Somewhere else. But my treat.'

She tosses her head. I can smell the lovely shampoo on her hair. 'I might be free on Saturday afternoon.'

'Right!' Wrong. I remember I'm working at Chalky's yard on Saturday. 'Oh no, I'm working!'

'Oh. Better forget it then.'

'No, how about Sunday instead?'

'Okay.'

'Cos if I work on Saturday I can afford to take you somewhere nice.'

'I said okay.'

'I mean I'm getting paid and –'

'Doogie! I already said okay!'

'You did? You said okay? You said yes?'

'Doogie, sometimes I wonder what planet you are on.'

22
· · · · · · ·

It's Sunday morning and the sky is blue and the birds are singing. Well, not singing: more like squawking since the only birds round our way are a few ragged crows pecking at road kill. They flap out of the way of my bicycle as I pedal towards Angelica's house. My muscles are aching from shovelling sand and gravel at Chalky's yard all day yesterday and we're going on a ten-mile bike ride, but I don't care. In fact I'm ecstatic because I know that later on today I'll get to kiss Angelica, and who knows what?

Angelica has decided she doesn't want to go to the cinema or to Café Vienna. She wants to do something different and she's chosen a bike ride and a picnic. DatingTips.com says you shouldn't let a girl decide what you're going to do on a date. DatingTips.com says that if a girl gets to decide then she's really just testing you to see if you're a pushover, and that really she wants you to brush aside her suggestions and tell her what's what. If you don't, it says, she will never respect you and will just laugh at you behind your back while she goes looking for a bloke who is more decisive. DatingTips.com says you should put your foot down with a firm hand.

I think DatingTips.com is full of crap.

I mean, how about she gets to choose this time and then you get to choose next time? That sounds like a better idea to me.

I deleted DatingTips.com from my list of favourites on my computer.

Anyway, we're going to cycle ten miles and have a picnic at a stone circle in the countryside. Angelica says it's a bit like Stonehenge only smaller. I've never been to a stone circle before and I'm quite curious about it, though I don't really know what you do when you get there. Maybe we throw a ball at it. I'm not going to dance around it that's for sure. Angelica can choose where we go but I draw the line at some things.

I arrive at Angelica's house. Her Dad is there in the driveway pumping air into the front tyre of her bicycle. It's the first time I've seen her folks since the evening when I stupidly thought that they had put a chip in my head. To tell the truth, I'm a bit embarrassed. Thankfully they don't know what was going on in my head, but there's still the thing about me snooping in the study.

I climb off my bike and hang back at the gateway.

He looks up. 'The Doogie! Hello. Come on in.' He bares his teeth at me. I know he means it to be a smile. It doesn't look like much of a smile though. I guess that he's still mad about catching me in his study. 'Bicycles,' he says, 'have a fantastic power-source-to-energy-propulsion ratio, don't you think?'

'Duh. Yeh.'

'Amazing. The ratio of input source to output source on a flat surface just makes you want to laugh, doesn't it?'

'Yeh. Ha. Haha.'

'Exactly. It makes you want to laugh and laugh. Bicycles, eh?'

I can't help it. My fingers touch the little scar on my head. Then I think: is he just pretending to have forgotten about being mad with me, or has he really forgotten? Then I think he really has forgotten. It's like he's just invented this bicycle.

'And it's efficient. Did you know that the conversion from calories to joules is 1 kilocalorie to 4180 J? Think about that!'

I nod my head, making out I'm impressed. Luckily Angelica and her Mum come outside and rescue me. 'Dominic!' shouts her mum. 'Are you boring the Doogie?'

'Not at all,' says Dominic. 'We were just analysing the mechanical advantage of this compound machine.'

'It's a bike, Dad,' says Angelica.

'I know that. You weren't bored, were you, the Doogie?'

'No,' I say.

'There you are: he wasn't bored at all.'

'Dad! He's just being polite.'

He turns to me, looking a bit puzzled and a bit cross. 'Why were you just being polite?'

'Dad!'

'Yes, leave the Doogie alone,' says Jennie. 'They want to get off on their ride!'

'Sorry!' he says. 'But it's all so interesting!'

At least they both genuinely seem to have forgotten or forgiven me for my behaviour last time I was at their house. Jennifer hands me a backpack with the picnic. I hope it's not sushi. Angelica climbs on her bike, and I get back on mine. We wave goodbye.

'Doesn't the motion transfer on a bicycle just make you want to laugh and laugh?' I hear Dominic say to Jennifer.

• • • •

It's good to get out of the town. We have a map to lead us through the country lanes and it really doesn't take us long to reach the field where the stone circle is. I'll be honest: it's not what I expected. There are about a dozen tall stones — mostly my height — stuck in the ground and forming a circle. The stones are called The Dancing Ladies because there is a legend about how they were ladies who were caught dancing on a Sunday and they were turned to stone. Maybe there was a rule that said you couldn't dance on a Sunday — I don't know. There is a small sign outside the field saying that these stones are known as The Dancing Ladies and that you should-n't damage them. That's it. That's all the information you get. You cycle more than ten miles and that's all you get told. That's rubbish. Rubbish in terms of information, I mean. What we need in life is more information about these things, not less.

There's nothing else there. I thought there might be an ice-cream van and a souvenir shop, and perhaps a couple of arcades with coin machines, that sort of thing. It would help it to be a bit more of a day out, that's all I'm saying. Angelica, though, loves it. I'm not saying it's bad. It's okay. I just don't love it as much as Angelica does.

She leans her bike against the fence and goes running inside. She goes up to the stones, brushing them with her hand as she walks round with half-closed eyes, almost in a dream.

'Fabulous isn't it?'

'Not bad,' I say.

'Not bad! It's four thousand years old!'

However old it is, we have it to ourselves. Angelica spreads a rug on the grass and we get out our picnic. The weather is surprisingly warm and luckily for us it turns out to be a beautiful day. The sun is shining down on the stones. They have an amber colour and the sunlight slides off them like honey. The grass at the foot of the stones is a brilliant emerald green. It all looks so good I think things might be starting to go right for a change.

We eat our sandwiches – not sushi – and wash them down with fruit smoothies. Then we lie on our backs on the picnic blanket, holding hands and looking up at the clouds. We play that game of seeing shapes and faces in the clouds. There's a whale, an angel, a unicorn; the usual type of thing.

Angelica squeezes my hand and I take that as a sign to roll over on my side and to kiss her. The kiss goes on for a long time. I find a way of kissing so that you don't even have to come up for air. We're inside that circle of golden stones on green, green grass and I feel just like I did that day in the park, but instead of the roundabout turning it feels like the stone circle is turning. Spinning very slowly. I think that would be right: the circle is turning, the earth is turning, the sun is turning, the universe is turning. Nothing you can do about it. Nothing you want to do about it.

I don't want the kissing to stop but of course it has to eventually. Then we just lie by each other's side in silence and I think I'm drifting off to sleep. I wonder what these ancient people were up to, sticking these stones in the earth like this. I wonder what it was all about.

Angelica is sleepy, too. I know she's drifting off. Maybe she's already gone. I pluck a straw of grass and try to tickle her ear with it, but she doesn't even feel it.

'What do you think it was for?' I say.

'Hmmm?'

'These stones in a circle.'

'Oh, it's what's left over,' she says dreamily. 'Let me snooze.'

'What?'

'From when the first ones came.'

'First ones?'

'They were like . . . launch pads. Landing bays. Very old technology . . . a few thousand years ago.'

I sit up. 'Eh? What are you talking about?'

Angelica suddenly sits up too. She has her hand over her mouth. 'Gosh. I was dreaming. Babbling in my sleep. Ignore me. It's just nonsense.' Then she lies down again and closes her eyes.

I look hard at her. Her eyes open. She looks back at me then closes her eyes again. The sun is beating down on her olive skin and making her hair shine like water. Her lips are like the buds of a flower. I shake my head and pretend that I didn't hear what she just said. I want to kiss her again, because whatever else she may be, she's a girl and she's beautiful.